THE OTHER MAN'S BLOOD
THE COMPLETE CASES OF THE
SCIENTIFIC CLUB, VOLUME 1

THE OTHER MAN'S BLOOD

THE COMPLETE CASES OF THE
SCIENTIFIC CLUB, VOLUME 1

RAY CUMMINGS

ILLUSTRATED BY
ROGER B. MORRISON

POPULAR PUBLICATIONS · 2022

TABLE OF CONTENTS

THE OTHER MAN'S BLOOD

1

SOME PRELIMINARY PROBLEMS

"**YOUR THEORY IS** certainly ingenious," laughed the Big Business Man. "I confess nothing of the kind has ever occurred to me."

"I did not mean to put it forth as particularly ingenious," replied the Brain Specialist seriously. "To me much of it seems quite obvious." He was evidently used to taking himself seriously, this eminent Alienist, yet he was not without a sense of humor, too, for his eyes twinkled as he looked around the clubroom at the interested little group of men, and continued: "If it does happen to be a fact, what funny things some of us must see."

The Playwright cleared a space before him on the table. "Let's get this straight," he said crisply. "This is great stuff." He look a silver coin from his pocket and laid it on the table with a click. "You say," he continued, addressing the Alienist, "that in all probability that half-dollar looks either larger or smaller to you than it does to me?"

"What I mean," replied the Alienist, "is that I do not believe that any of the five senses of any individual are affected in the same way by external things. I do not think that there is any standard to which we all conform. On the contrary, it is my opinion that the standard is different for each one of us."

"All right," said the Playwright, and laid a smaller coin on the table beside the first. "That much is clear."

"Not clear at all," laughed the Big Business Man.

"Aw shut up, Will," said the Playwright. "Give us a chance, will you?"

The Alienist moved his chair up to the table beside the Playwright. "What you want to get at," he said, "is how big those coins look to me."

"Yes," said the Playwright.

"Let me put it the other way," returned the Alienist. "How big do they look to you?"

The Playwright thought a moment. "That half-dollar," he said slowly, "looks about an inch and a quarter in diameter, and the dime about half that or more."

"You mean," said the Alienist, "you think that's the size they are. As a matter of fact, I believe you're right—those are about their actual measurements. But you're wrong if you think they look that large to you now. How big is an inch and a quarter?"

The Playwright held up his thumb and forefinger.

"All right," continued the Alienist, "Now, honestly, does that half-dollar look that big to you? Measure it with your eye." Then he laughed at the puzzled expression on the Playwright's face, and went on.

"Of course it doesn't—not half as big, does it?"

The Playwright agreed that it did not.

The Big Business Man, sitting further back from the table, also had been studying the coins earnestly through his extended thumb and forefinger.

"I think you're off on that line of argument," he began. "That half-dollar looks pretty small to me here. But that is

only because I am so far away from it. If I get closer—" He
rose as he spoke and took a step toward the table. "Now it
looks much larger. And if I get right up to it"—he put his
fingers down on the coin—"it looks its full size—an inch
and a quarter. It's only a question of how far away you are,"
he finished, somewhat triumphantly.

"I felt sure one of you would think of that," said the
Alienist. "You're quite right as far as you go. We are all of us
agreed that the dime is a little more than half the diameter
of the half-dollar. And also we agree that the farther away
we get the smaller things look. Relative size is, I am sure,
the same with us all. But absolute apparent size is quite a
different matter."

After a moment of silence he continued: "The point is,
we have all of us accepted a standard of measurement. We
call it so many inches or feet. We know what an inch or a
foot looks like to us, and we gauge the relative size of things
by that. And so, of course, we all agree that a thing is of
the same dimensions, more or less, because we all have the
same ability to estimate its size relative to the standard of
measurement. But the point is, how do we know the inch
looks the same to both of us? That would make all the
difference in the world, wouldn't it?"

"An inch looks that big to me," said the Very Young
Man, holding up his thumb and forefinger.

"Yes, it does to me, too," laughed the Alienist. "But
how do you know how big your hand looks to me, or
the space between your fingers? For all you know, if you
could suddenly see that hand with my eyes you'd think it
belonged to a giant, and you'd call that space two or three
inches—or perhaps a yard—who knows?"

"If I may be allowed to suggest—" began the Country Doctor timidly. He was a jovially rotund little man, with side whiskers and spectacles well down on his nose. He was a visitor at the club.

"Go right ahead, Bert," said the Alienist, "you probably know as much about this as any of us."

The Country Doctor looked quizzically around at the company with eyes that twinkled over the top rims of his glasses. "I've treated lots of people in my time. More than you have, I guess," he said, turning to his friend the Alienist. "I was just going to say that if ever one of my patients talked the way you do, I'd humor him very carefully, give him a pill, and hope for the best."

The Alienist laughed. "All right, Bert," he said. "Give me one of your pills, it won't hurt me any, I know." Then, with a sudden thought, he went over to the window and raised the shade. "There's the full moon," he said. "Come here just a moment." The Big Business Man and the Playwright came.

"Now," said the Alienist, putting his hands on their shoulders and stepping back out of the way, "look at that moon, look at it carefully. How big does it look?"

"Half a dollar."

"A dinner plate." They spoke almost simultaneously.

"There you are, gentlemen," laughed the Alienist, turning back to the room. " 'Half a dollar'—'a dinner plate,' they say. We take something for which there is no common, familiar, relative standard of measurement, which is at a comparatively great distance away, and one estimates its apparent diameter to be ten times as great as the other."

The Banker had not moved from his chair nor spoken

since the argument began. Now, as the three men turned back from the window, he laid down his cigar and reached for a push-button in the wall. "Let's have a drink," he suggested, waving his hand toward the room at large, "you people are dry enough, you ought to be thirsty."

"Much obliged George," laughed the Big Business Man, "we admit the thirst."

"Speaking of thirst—" said the Playwright.

"That's all right," said the Big Business Man, "George is always speaking of thirst."

"What I was going to say," went on the Playwright, blandly ignoring the interruption, "I suppose your theory extends to the sense of taste also." He turned to the Alienist. "Do you believe we taste things differently, too?"

"Why not?" replied the Alienist. "Taste is certainly as individual as sight. I think it very probable that even the basic fundamentals of taste are quite different in each of us."

The Playwright thought a moment. "Then is it possible that what tastes sweet to me tastes sour to you?" he asked.

"Quite possible, yes," replied the Alienist.

"Wait a moment, gentlemen, don't let's go so fast," protested the Big Business Man. "You say, perhaps, what tastes sweet to some of us might taste sour to others? How does a lemon taste to you?" He addressed the Playwright.

"Sour," said the Playwright.

"Acid," said the Banker, "rotten taste."

"And you—and you." The Big Business Man indicated the others in turn. They all agreed that it tasted "acidly sour."

"Very well," finished the Big Business Man, "we all agree we think we know what a lemon tastes like, at any rate."

"You put it very well," said the Alienist. "We think we know what a lemon tastes like. Whatever taste it is that a lemon gave to our sense when we first tried one, we have all learned to call 'sour.' So we all agree a lemon has a sour taste. As a matter of fact, to me it may taste what you would call sweet. When I first tasted a lemon as a child, or anything similar, no matter what sensation I got from the taste, I was taught to call it sour. And I've been calling it sour ever since. But that does not mean that what you were taught to call sour is the same taste. Not at all."

"Then maybe custard pie tastes like apple," shouted the Playwright hilariously; "and pea soup tastes like tomato, and—and—"

"And I'll bet you like raw oysters with sugar, only you don't know it," put in the Very Young Man.

The Banker raised both his arms in protest.

"Gentlemen, gentlemen!" he cried testily, above the din of shouts and laughter. "For the love of Heaven cut out that stuff. I've listened to a lot of weird arguments in this club, but this one is the most asinine, idiotic—"

2

THE MAN IN THE CASE

THE PLAYWRIGHT ROSE to his feet suddenly. "Gentlemen, one moment," he interrupted with a melodramatic gesture. "I have a question to ask. We have heard this gentleman,"—he indicated the Alienist—"expound a most interesting theory. We have tried to disprove it—we have failed. But, I rise to ask you, why are these extraordinary things so?" He waxed eloquently enthusiastic. "We believe they are so, but why—I ask you all, why?" He sat down abruptly and took a drink.

"That's philosophy," laughed the Big Business Man.

"All right," said the Playwright, "what if it is? Nothing's too complicated for us."

"I think I can help you out on that," began the Alienist seriously. The room became quiet in a moment. "You're right. It is philosophy when you search for the reason why are these differences. Red and green, for instance, are probably quite reversed in the perception of some of us. Yet the shapes of objects, I venture to say, are unchanged. Color changes, sound changes, but shape does not. Now philosophy teaches that there is a fundamental difference between these two classes. Color and sound are dependent for their very existence on our human senses. Without eyes to see, there can be no color; without ears to hear, there can be no sound. But substance and shape are not dependent on human senses for their existence."

"Why not?" interrupted the Playwright, "According to your own argument, if there is nobody to touch a substance it does not exist. That seems the same reasoning to me."

"That makes you an egoist. Are you an egoist?" demanded the Big Business Man accusingly.

The Playwright looked bewildered. "Am I—am I a what?" he stammered.

"What a rotten thing to be," said the Banker, and they all laughed at the Playwright's confusion.

"That does make you an egoist," said the Alienist. "They believed—Berkeley was their leader, you know—that nothing exists except in the mind. I disagree with them. I draw the line at what we generally term material things. Therefore to me it seems even more logical than ever to suppose that what is dependent on our senses for its very existence should he interpreted differently by each of us, while that which is independent of us, remains constant. Do I make myself clear?"

"Well," answered the Playwright slowly, "I shouldn't like to say your conversation bubbled with the crystal clarity of a mountain spring. But I think I'm with you."

The Country Doctor cleared his throat ostentatiously, and looked as though he wanted to speak but didn't dare.

"Come on Bert," said the Alienist, "you look as though you had something important to add to our argument."

"I haven't," said the Country Doctor; "you've been way out of my depth ever since you started. What I was going to ask was where you all got these unearthly ideas? I know it is your business to pretend to understand all the funny things that get the matter with people's brains, but I didn't think you'd get that way yourself."

"Nonsense, Bert," laughed his friend, "you never appreciated me, that's all. Why, I'll tell you," he went on seriously; "that theory was first suggested to my mind by a curious case of blood transfusion listed by Dr. Ralph in the Journal of the English Society of Medical Research, ten years or more, now, I guess it was. The case was most extraordinary. Something similar, but in an infinitely lesser degree, has happened in other transfusion cases, I understand, but nothing of enough importance to be recorded. This case was unique; nobody could explain it. Whether it ever was explained, I do not know. But it interested me tremendously, and as I got thinking it over, the theories about which we have been arguing came to me as a possible explanation. I'll tell you about the case if you like."

"Go on—do," they exclaimed in unison.

"It isn't a very long story," began the Alienist, "but to my mind it certainly is full of possibilities."

There was a stir in the room as they all drew their chairs closer to the Alienist and prepared to listen.

"I used to know Dr. Ralph in Paris—I have seen him perform one or two of his transfusion operations," began the Alienist again. "I was always mildly interested in that sort of thing. Then Dr. Ralph went to London. He was at the height of his fame about that time.

"One day I picked up a year-old copy of the Journal of the English Society for Medical Research, and listed among Dr. Ralph's transfusion cases was the one I have mentioned. The patient was named Jones—Charles Jones,

I think. He was a man around thirty. The blood was given by an older man friend of his. The operation was satisfactory—quite the usual one, in fact.

"The extraordinary part of the case was that when the patient came from under the anesthetic his intelligence was absolutely gone. He had become an idiot, unable to speak words, or to understand words. So far as the record showed, this man Jones had been quite a normal individual, suffering only from anemia that necessitated the operation. There was no reason to suppose his brain was diseased. Yet this blood transfusion completely destroyed his reason; no paresis, however advanced, could have affected him more completely. His helplessness, his mouthing, hideous attempts to speak were in fact all characteristic of the idiocy of paresis.

"That is in substance all the report gave. Only one other point I remember seemed to me of the utmost significance. Dr. Ralph mentioned that at times the man's eyes seemed to shine with an almost uncanny intelligence, as though there was something back of them that he was trying to communicate, but couldn't."

The Alienist stopped speaking. The room remained quite silent. "That's all," he said finally.

"Gosh," said the Very Young Man, helping himself to another of the Playwright's cigarettes, "you give me the creeps."

For some moments no one spoke. Then the Big Business Man drained his glass, lighted a cigar, and moved his chair forward nearer the Alienist.

"I think I see what you mean," he began. In spite of his apparent effort to control it his voice trembled. "Your idea is that this Jones, through the transfusion of blood, saw, heard, and felt things, not in the way to which he had been accustomed, but with the senses of the friend who had furnished the blood?"

"Yes," said the Alienist, "that's just about what I mean."

The Playwright jumped to his feet. "Good Lord!" he began excitedly, "then according to that everything must have been so totally different that he couldn't recognize anything!"

"I think that's the explanation," said the Alienist quietly. "We must assume that for some unexplainable reason this particular transfusion of blood carried with it into Jones's brain the other man's individual interpretation of the external world, and at the same time nullified and overcame all the perceptions to which Jones's senses had become accustomed. Assuming this, it follows that if the original differences of perception were great enough between these two individuals, Jones's intelligence would be completely destroyed.

"In fact, with a set of circumstances as we have constructed them, it follows quite logically that the result would be similar to that which actually transpired in Jones's case."

"Let's get this straight," said the Playwright. "It's too big for me—it's making me dizzy."

"If you'll excuse me for saying so," began the Country Doctor, "it's an awful wild theory, but it seems to me that since you gentlemen have accepted all the rest, to blame it on blood transfusion ought not to be too much for your credulity." He beamed on them with a little superior air, belied by the twinkle in his eye.

"I can easily imagine how it would be," said the Big Business Man. "This man Jones came out of the anesthetic and found that every word he tried to use fitted wrongly. Everything he saw looked strange; everything he heard sounded differently; everything tasted differently. Why it must have been as though he were in another world. No wonder he couldn't understand, or make himself understood."

"And no wonder his eyes looked intelligent and pleading," said the Playwright.

The Banker shuddered quite visibly. "You people make me sick," he growled to hide his feelings. "What is the use of all this, anyway? You're getting yourselves all worked up over nothing. Maybe what you say is possible; Heaven knows I'd hate to bet on it. But what's the use, you can't prove it, you know."

"Of course we can't prove it," said the Playwright. "But it's great stuff to talk about, anyhow. Some day I'm going to write a—

"I think it's damn rot!" said the Banker.

Unnoticed by the interested little group of men gathered around the table under the light, the figure of a man detached itself from the shadows in a corner of the room, and advanced toward them.

"Gentlemen, I—I hope you'll pardon me," began the stranger in a mildly apologetic tone. "I could not very well help overhearing you. I have been sitting there." He indicated a chair close by to the wall.

As he came within the circle of light they saw he was a negligible-looking little man, forty or forty-five perhaps, slender of build, a pale face, pale-blue eyes, and thin, light blond hair. His smile as he spoke was pleasant; his whole personality was rather pleasing than otherwise. Yet he was so unforceful, so drab in both looks and demeanor that one would never have thought of looking at him twice.

The Playwright made way for him courteously, and indicated a vacant chair near at hand.

"We're glad to have you join us," he said pleasantly. "We think, that is, nearly all of us"—he looked at the Banker and grinned—"think we're having quite an interesting little argument."

"It has been very interesting to me," said the little man.

"They think they've got a lot of wonderful ideas," said the Banker. "Easy enough to dope out weird stuff like that when there's no possible way of proving whether you're right or not."

"It has been very interesting to me," repeated the little man in a low tone, as though talking to himself. Then he looked from one to the other of the faces around him.

"I suppose, gentlemen," he went on. "I suppose I ought to—I hope you'll pardon me for interfering—" He spoke most apologetically. "Your conversation has been most interesting to me, because I—you see, I'm Charles Jones. I'm the man you've been talking about."

3

THE FACTS OF THE CASE

THE EFFECT OF this quiet statement upon the company was extraordinary. The appearance of the newcomer was so insignificant and his manner of speaking so mild, so almost timidly apologetic, that it greatly enhanced by contrast the effect of his words.

The Playwright, the Big Business Man and the Very Young Man all started talking at once. It was the Very Young Man who first made himself heard. "Why, he knows all about it, he knows all about everything," he almost shouted.

The little man sat down suddenly in the chair that had been offered him and seemed embarrassed at being so suddenly thrust into the center of the stage.

"Well, George, what do you say to that?" said the Big Business Man, turning to the Banker triumphantly. "I guess we can prove some of these theories now all right. This is the man we've been talking about; he's the man who knows all about it."

The Banker grinned back at him sarcastically. "Oh, all right," he said, "if this really is the same Charles Jones who lost his brains because he had a blood transfusion we'll get a fine chance to find out what a lot of bunk your theories are."

"Gee, you got a mean disposition!" murmured the Very Young Man, and then promptly looked very much relieved when nobody heard him but the Playwright, who winked solemnly.

"I'm the same Charles Jones," said the newcomer wearily. "I was Dr. Ralph's patient in 1908 and my—my head did go wrong."

"Will you tell us about it?" asked the Alienist gently. There was something about this inoffensive little man that made them want to treat him kindly. "We want to hear your story, naturally," he added.

"Are they right about things all looking so differently? Is that what was the matter with you?" asked the Very Young Man eagerly.

"Yes," answered Jones, and put his hands over his eyes. "That's what was the matter with me."

"Then our theories really do explain your case?" said the Playwright.

"They explain it, yes," said Jones, "You had the general idea about right, only it was a thousand times more horrible—more horrible—" His voice trailed away into silence, and again he buried his face in his hands.

"Give him a drink," said the Banker gruffly. "He looks as if he needed it."

The Very Young Man hurried out of the room and was back in an incredibly short time with a whisky and soda.

"Here," he said, offering it. Jones drank gratefully, and then looked around with his sad smile. "It's very good of you all, gentlemen," he said. "I'll tell my story if you want me to. I've never told it very often. I'm all alone—I haven't many friends. And then, too, you see it—it hurts very much to do it."

"Pass it up," said the Banker, "we understand," and the others assented.

"I'll tell it," said Jones. "You've almost earned the right to hear it, since apparently you are the only ones who ever worked out the explanation of what really happened to me."

"He did it," said the Very Young Man, pointing to the Alienist.

"The reason it hurts," went on Jones, drawing a deep breath and speaking so low they could hardly hear him, "is because it made me—made me lose my wife. And I haven't anybody else—so you see, I'm all alone," he finished and smiled again wistfully.

"Where's that waiter?" roared the Banker, breaking the silence that followed. "I pushed that button three times in five minutes and nothing happens. This is a rotten club."

The Very Young Man jumped up and pushed the button again violently.

"All I'm doing now is just looking further," said Jones in the same low voice. "Just looking for her, because, you see. I don't—I don't know where she is."

"You want to tell us all about it," suggested the Alienist.

"I'll tell you all about it—from the beginning," said the little man. "You see, all I'm doing now is looking for her, and for him. I want to find him, too," he finished. He sat up in his chair abruptly, his eyes gleaming with a new light, and a bright red spot glowing in each of his pale cheeks.

"I'll be right back," said the Very Young Man. "I want to get that waiter. Please don't start till I get back."

Again the men settled themselves comfortably in their chairs, and prepared to listen. The Very Young Man returned in a moment with a much chastened waiter, and after the drinks had been ordered, Charles Jones began his narrative. He sat hunched forward in a big leather chair, just beyond the direct glare of the center drop light. He spoke in a low, even voice, with a preoccupied air, his tones calmly dispassionate, yet with a curious quality of repression. And from time to time, as he spoke of his wrongs, there gleamed again in his eyes that incongruous fire that none of his hearers quite understood.

"I am, or rather I was," he began, "a teacher of history. Twelve years ago, when I was twenty-eight, I became a member of the faculty of Rexford College, England. I am an American by birth, but I spent much of my boyhood in England, and was educated there. I was always in rather delicate health. I studied too much, I suppose. They used to call me the Bookworm in school." He paused a moment, smiled; then went on:

"I met the girl—whom I whom I afterward made my wife, just about the time I went to Rexford. She was an English girl, six years younger than I." He stopped again, and moistened his lips.

"Was she pretty?" asked the Very Young Man impulsively, and immediately looked sorry he had spoken.

Charles Jones flushed a little, and again he smiled his weary smile. "Very pretty—yes. Everyone said that."

"You're an impertinent fool!" said the Banker gruffly to

the Very Young Man, and the Very Young Man looked as though he agreed with him heartily.

"We were married in 1907," resumed Jones, "about a year after I took up my duties at Rexford. We were very happy, only we—only we didn't have any children. Now I thank God for that!"

The Very Young Man parted his lips as if to speak. Then, meeting the Banker's glance, closed them again.

"We didn't have many friends, I'm not much at that sort of thing, and I was greatly absorbed in my work, and—and in her. I know now she must have found it terribly dull in that little town—she was a London girl, you see.

"We only had one real friend. His name was Willard Blackstone. He was professor of chemistry at Rexford. We used to see him a great deal, we—we both liked him very much.

"In the winter of 1907 my health begin to fail. I was always anemic, and at this time I grew rapidly worse.

"For several months I was treated by the local doctor at Rexford. I don't think my condition was particularly alarming and while I did not show any especial improvement, still I certainly did not get any worse. During almost all this time I remember, Blackstone was urging me to consult Dr. Ralph in London and to have a—to have a blood transfusion. He offered to undergo it with me, he was a remarkably robust man. He convinced me and the Rexford doctor that it would do me an immense amount of good.

"We went to London together to see Dr. Ralph. He told me such an operation was not absolutely necessary, but since my friend stood ready to furnish the blood which

Dr. Ralph examined and found satisfactory, he was sure the result would be beneficial.

"I decided finally to have the operation, and a month later, my—my wife and I, with Willard Blackstone, went back to London. The transfusion was performed by Dr. Ralph in November, 1908, at the Memorial Hospital, in London."

Jones stopped, and looked around at his audience with a helpless air. They shifted expectantly in their chairs, some of them, but no one spoke.

"Gentlemen, I—I hardly know how to go on." Jones resumed after a moment. "It is very difficult to put it into words. I took the anesthetic and I think—I think I went under it very hard. I don't know whether the sensations I felt were while I was losing consciousness or regaining it, but I do know that I was tortured by the feeling of a most horrible struggle within me. It was more than physical or mental torture—it was as if my soul were fighting—fighting a battle for its very existence. I seemed to be every fiber in me seemed to be striving to combat some terrible evil.

"What's the use, gentlemen? What I say must convey so little to you, yet even now, after all these years, it seems so plain to me. The memories are so vivid—so vivid."

His voice trailed away again, and he stopped.

"You were regaining consciousness, probably," said the Alienist quietly.

"Why, what he is telling us," exclaimed the Big Business Man, "must be the battle of his soul trying to ward off the influence that came with the other man's blood."

"Yes," said the Alienist. "What he is trying to describe is undoubtedly the result of this sudden usurpation by an alien influence of all the sensations his being had always held. God knows how we can understand, or even imagine the tremendous forces that must have been at work to effect this change."

"It was so horrible—so horrible," began Jones again, "and it seemed to last an eternity. For countless years—much longer, very much longer than all the memories of my whole lifetime, it seemed to go on. Finally I opened my eyes." He stopped abruptly. Then after a long silence he resumed.

"You'll have to excuse me, gentlemen, if what I say seems incoherent. I am trying to put my thoughts into words that will mean something to you. My thoughts are very clear—very vivid to me, but somehow there do not seem to be any words to fit them. Can you understand that?"

"I've had it with dreams," said the Playwright, "you wake up and remember you've been dreaming. It is quite tangible in your mind, but if you start telling it to someone it just seems to fade away, and what you say sounds foolish. I've had that often."

"It seems to me quite logical," said the Alienist, "that since the very essence of this matter lies in the fact that everything became so changed that words were of no use, it is the most natural thing in the world to suppose that he would have difficulty in fitting words now to the impression he is trying to convey to us."

"That's just the way it is," said the little man, "it seems just beyond the border of tangible words—it's very elusive. I opened my eyes, and what I saw at first was a sort of—well, I suppose I shall have to call it just a gray mist. As far as I could see for—for illimitable distances there was a gray expanse of mist rolling and trembling. Then out of the fog, shapes began to take form. I saw the dim outlines of a room gradually closing in around me, all obscured in places by the fog. At first these shadowy outlines seemed vague, unreal and unstable—just floating in through the fog. Then as I stared the fog seemed gradually to dissolve. The room became steady and took on an appearance of reality. Only, the fog never entirely lifted; it hung like a veil between me and the room and in places it was so dense as to entirely obscure parts of the scene. I recognized the room at once; it was the room in the hotel near the hospital where my wife was staying."

Jones stopped again, and looked around at his audience. His face was flushed a little now, and his eyes sparkled with animation. He took another sip of his drink and waited, obviously expecting someone to question him.

The Playwright was the first to speak. "I'm afraid I don't get you at all," he began.

"Neither do I," interrupted the Very Young Man.

"I thought our whole theory," went on the Playwright, "was that after this blood transfusion you saw things so differently that you couldn't recognize anything—that your intelligence was unable to cope with the new world as you saw it. Now you tell us about a room you recognized at once. It's very confusing."

"You said it," remarked the Very Young Man.

Jones looked apologetic. "I'm afraid I'm a very bad story-teller," he said, smiling. "I quite forgot to mention that while your theories are correct in their way, they are very incomplete. There was something else happened to me, far more—more revolutionary—something none of you have mentioned."

"What was it?" asked the Very Young Man eagerly.

"I thought," went on Jones, disregarding the interruption, "that the best way was to tell you just what my impressions were. You can fit in the explanation as we go along." He looked at the Alienist.

"Tell it your own way," said the Alienist. "I think I see—"

"Let me ask you this," interrupted the Big Business Man. "We are all to understand, aren't we, that when you first opened your eyes, you were in the hospital—that the real tangible world about you was so changed in every way as to be invisible?"

"Yes," said Jones, "practically so—at the first, anyway."

"Then the hotel room you describe—that was a hallucination, a vision?"

"What I actually saw of the hospital appeared only a—a gray fog," replied Jones, "what I thought I saw was—was the hold room—"

"I don't exactly get that," said the Playwright.

"Never mind," replied the Alienist. "Go on," he added, "tell your story your own way."

"I can remember lying for a long time looking at the fog and the room. I seemed to be in the room now, for it had entirely closed in around me. The fog still hung down like a veil in front of me, and the heavy opaque patches rolled and tumbled about, hiding first one part, and then another, of everything within my range of vision.

"Suddenly I became aware of a figure, sitting in a chair by the window. It was my wife. And as the fog cleared away in front of her, I met her eyes looking over at me. They were filled with tears. Then she smiled pathetically. I tried to sit up in bed. I think I did sit up. The feeling was indescribably horrible. Then I spoke, and from my throat I heard issue unintelligible gibberish—hardly human, even in its into- nation. Yet I knew I had spoken words—somehow amid all this phantasmagoria. I seemed to know I was quite sane. Oddly enough, too, I was not particularly frightened.

"My wife, quite obviously, could not hear my voice. Her eyes looked straight at me, but she gave no sign. The fog drifted past her for a moment. Then it cleared again. As it did so, suddenly the whole room shifted downward several feet. It seemed to drop down noiselessly and smoothly. Then it slid toward me, widening out as it came, until my wife, still sitting quietly in her chair, was quite close to me. I seemed to be hovering in the air two or three feet above her and directly in front. As the room came to rest, she looked up into my eyes, and smiled again sadly. Then she spoke, directly to me this time.

"What do they say now?" she asked in a low voice.

"She was looking at me, not through me; yet I knew it was not I to whom she was speaking. And then I heard another voice—a voice I recognized at once as Willard Blackstone's—saying:

" 'It is as they feared, little woman; he's hopelessly insane.' "

"Gentlemen, I hope you will understand me when I say that now all at once I realized fully the meaning of these fantastic visions. For the voice of Blackstone seemed to come from me. And I knew, quite definitely I knew, it did not come from me."

"Good God," muttered the Banker, as silence fell upon the little group of intent listeners.

4

THE PSYCHIC BOND

IT WAS SOME moments before anyone in the room spoke. Jones lay back in his chair, overcome seemingly with the emotion his memories aroused. The others sat staring at him blankly, too amazed for words. Only the Alienist retained a measure of composure. He smoked on quietly, apparently piecing together the new ideas as he heard them into the fabric of another theory reconcilable with that he had already formed. He was the first to speak.

"Gentlemen," he began quietly, "some of you probably have not been able to interpret clearly the things Mr. Jones has been telling us, or to reconcile his experiences with the theories we were discussing before he was good enough to make himself known to us."

"You said it," murmured the Very Young Man again.

"In order that we may all be able to understand perfectly his narrative," went on the Alienist, "and keep it free from the confusion of misunderstanding, I think I ought to give you my theoretical interpretations of what we have heard so far. Mr. Jones can check me up if I go wrong."

They all nodded assent to this proposition, and the Alienist continued:

"First of all, gentlemen, let us go back to our original

theory. We decided that since the other man's blood in Jones gave him so utterly different a viewpoint, he could not fit in with the world as he saw it in any way. Hence he became, to all outward appearances, an idiot.

"Now, that theory still holds good. We do not even have to modify it. So far as he has gone, he represents the world as he actually saw it—merely as a gray fog, colorless, formless, soundless. I can well imagine that in the first effort of his senses to adapt themselves to a flood of new impressions, they would fail utterly to interpret anything. It is quite conceivable to picture the result as he has described it.

"So much for that. Am I right, Jones?"

"Quite right—yes," said Jones with a sigh.

"Now, to add to our former theory," went on the Alienist, we have to consider another fundamental change—a change, I must confess, had never occurred to me, but which certainly seems perfectly obvious when once you think of it.

"We assumed that with the coming of the other man's blood would come this different interpretation of the outside world; but we did not assume that with the blood would come the ability to see the world from the other man's viewpoint—with his eyes, interpreted with his mind, so to speak."

"I don't get you," said the Playwright. "Say that again."

The Alienist smiled. "I'm afraid I'm meeting with Jones's difficulty," he said. "Words do seem rather inadequate to convey ideas such as these. What I mean is this. When Jones saw that room, he saw it from the viewpoint of Willard Blackstone. It was what Blackstone's eyes were seeing at that particular instant. When he thought his wife was looking at him, it was Blackstone at whom she was looking, to whom she spoke, and who spoke to her."

"And when the room slid downward, and then came forward," said the Playwright, "it must have been that Blackstone got up and walked across it. That would change Jones's viewpoint the way he describes, wouldn't it?"

"I've seen it that way on a railroad train," began the Very Young Man. "You look out of the window at a train on the next track, and all at once you think your train has started forward. But it hasn't; the other train has started the other way. But it looks the same to you."

"That's a good illustration," said the Alienist. "Are we right about all this, Jones?"

"Quite right—yes," said Jones again, with the same hopeless air.

The Banker suddenly pushed his chair violently backward, and sat up very straight, with a most determinedly belligerent manner.

"Now, look here," he began, addressing nobody in particular. "I like a good, honest argument. And, as most of you know, I'm not averse to swallowing a few wild theories upon occasion. I'm not a scientific man by nature; but since I've been a member of this club, these past six years, I've had a lot of science thrust upon me.

"Oh, I know I've had to accept some weird ideas as true—I've had them proved on me. I admit it," he added, at the smile on the Big Business Man's face.

"I really think," he went on, "that by now I'm an expert scientist. But right here I balk. With all due respect to you, sir"—he turned to Jones as he spoke—"you people are just hypnotizing yourselves into believing a lot of bunk. Something happened to our little friend here. Far be it from me to deny that; but just what happened, I'm blessed if I can find out. But one thing I do know: I can shoot your theories full of holes without half trying."

He sat back, trying to appear indignant, but only succeeding in looking his usual complacent self.

"Go ahead, George, shoot," said the Big Business Man.

"Well, in the first place," began the Banker, "here's Jones lying in bed in a hospital. He has some of another man's blood in him. All right. I can imagine that possibly it might change him in some way. It's even conceivable that he might think things, or even see things, that the other man had thought or had seen when the blood was in him. But for the love of Heaven how can you possibly imagine that while lying in that bed he would see things happening at the same time in quite another place? I don't understand how the blood's got anything to do with that."

"Why not?" asked the Very Young Man

"Why has it?" retorted the Banker.

"Why hasn't it?" said the Very Young Man.

"Why not treacle?" laughed the Playwright. "You talk like 'Alice in Wonderland.'"

The Banker threw himself back in his chair and shrugged his shoulders. "You people have got 'Alice in Wonderland' skinned a mile," he said. "You're hopeless."

"I think your argument is quite all right," said the Alienist. "You have mentioned the great basic difference in the two theories. Our first one allowed the assumption of the physical presence of the new blood only accounting for the change. Now we must admit something which is far less tangible."

"Call it psychic," said the Playwright.

"That's just what I would call it," answered the Alienist. "It doesn't seem to me incredible that with the coming of this new blood would come a new—let us say, personality—mingled with and warring with the old. And with the establishment of this dominating personality, surely it is not a far cry to imagine a psychic bond being created between the two individuals. Call it thought transference, if you will. We admit thought transference has occurred between individuals entirely disassociated. How much more likely that it would occur in such a case as this."

"Have it your own way," said the Banker; "only I know—"

"It occurs to me," interrupted the Big Business Man thoughtfully, "that it is somewhat peculiar all this should have happened in this case, when so many other blood transfusions have been made without any such phenomena."

"It beats me," remarked the Playwright.

"I know why it happened to me," said Jones, and again his eyes gleamed strangely and his cheeks burned red, "I know why it happened, but I don't know how—I mean exactly what caused it."

"Why did it happen to you?" asked the Playwright.

"I—I you'll understand when—" he stopped.

"Couldn't we go on with the story?" suggested the Very Young Man.

5

THROUGH THE EYES OF ANOTHER

"**WHEN I FIRST** realized," resumed Jones earnestly, that the
voice of Willard Blackstone was in some way associated
with me and with my—my personality, so to speak, I found
myself torn by the most conflicting emotions it probably
has ever been the misfortune of a human mind to face. My
body was lying in the hospital bed—of that fact I seemed
positive. My eyes saw the real world only as an expanse of
fog rolling and tumbling about. My lips spoke gibberish,
my ears heard only a faint, indeterminate hum of vague,
unfamiliar sounds hopelessly mingled and confused.

"But beyond all that, I seemed to have acquired a new
being. I saw this hotel-room now, after a few moments, as
plainly as though I were in it. I heard Willard Blackstone
speaking with a voice that seemed to come from me. I
knew I was seeing what his eyes saw. And then suddenly
I found myself thinking thoughts that I knew were his
thoughts."

Jones stopped again for a moment.

"I am not going to try, gentlemen," he continued finally,
"to make you understand the flood of impressions that
now overcame me. I was filled with horror at the thoughts,
the knowledge that suddenly loosed itself upon my intel-

ligence. I can remember that none of this seemed queer at the time. I accepted it all as being quite a reasonable state of affairs. Only I was—was horrified at what I knew, and at my—my own helplessness to combat it.

"For some time my wife and Blackstone talked together. 'He has recovered consciousness,' I heard him tell her. 'It's as they feared—he's hopelessly insane.'

"Gentlemen, can I make you understand that as I heard him say this, and as I saw my wife's face whiten and her eyes fill up, I—I knew what he was thinking. Through my brain, dimly but clearly, were going the same thoughts that were in his. And I knew then that he did not think me insane, that he knew or believed my condition to be similar to what it actually was.

"I listened to them talk for a while. Then their voices grew fainter. The scene faded gradually, as though the fog were growing deeper and blotting it out. Then I became acutely conscious of my body lying in bed. Then came the silence and blackness of oblivion.

"The next thing I knew was opening my eyes upon the interior of a railway carriage. I caught a faint glimpse of my wife sitting beside me in the compartment. I heard Blackstone's voice, coming from me, speak to her. Then my ears were filled with a horrible, incoherent jargon of detached words, the fog rolled up again and blotted the train from my sight all except one little corner that persisted dimly visible, fading and brightening alternately.

"Again I became aware of my body lying in bed; felt it more tangible this time, with an extraordinary sensation for which I have no words of description. The jargon—I suppose I may as well call it that—still roared in my ears, and the gray fog rolled about thicker and darker than ever before.

Only now the fog seemed to be forming itself into shapes. I blinked at it for a moment, dazed, and found before me a huge, irregular outline that finally I perceived to be a nurse. In outline of form she was, shall I say, human? She seemed nearly ten feet tall, as she stood there beside me. Yet, curiously enough, I found that I did not have to look up to her any more than if she were of normal height. I shifted my glance away, and made out the footboard of the bed in which I was lying. It, too, was gigantic in size. Then I saw the dim outlines of the room, enormous in proportion, yet all seemingly in perfect adjustment with my vision.

"The nurse was dressed in white. I looked into her face. It was ghastly white, with a greenish tinge, and the cheeks were flushed with a greenish purple. I closed my eyes, shuddering.

"Again I heard that strange, roaring sound in my ears. A wave of air struck my hot, feverish face, and I felt a horrible touch of something pressing down upon my forehead, and then back over my hair. I held myself tense with eyes tightly closed, thrilling with—with fear at the feeling.

"I say fear, gentlemen. It wasn't fear. I don't know what it was. And I don't know how to describe that touch upon my head. It was horrible only at first because of its unfamiliarity. After a moment I found it not unpleasant.

"I opened my eyes again. The gigantic nurse was still standing beside me. I could see her arm stretching down toward my face, and then I knew it was her hand I felt upon my forehead. I looked into her face. Her purple lips were parting; I could see the gleam of her white teeth behind.

Then she spoke, in a great, roaring voice like an animal. I could make out the separation of words, but as I have analyzed it since I realize that nothing was familiar save an occasional individual syllable.

"Then I saw in her other hand a glass of water—I suppose it was water. It looked like water, save that it reflected purple from the flesh of her hand holding the glass. She offered it to me, and I drank. The liquid sparkled down my throat like champagne, biting my palate and tongue with its sharpness. I choked a little and pushed the glass away. Some of the water spilled upon my hand. It seemed to eat into the flesh like an acid, but when I wiped it away the sensation was gone, replaced by the equally unfamiliar one of the touch of my hand against the bedclothes.

"I flung myself back on the bed, and watched the figure of the nurse as she drew back into the obscurity of the farther distance of the room.

"Gentlemen, I don't see much sense in my keeping on telling you these impressions. They only confirm, more in detail, of course, the theories about which you were arguing a while ago. For several weeks I lay in that hospital bed, as I now know, under the interested and puzzled scrutiny of the greatest specialists in England at that time.

"During these weeks, and the months following them that I spent in the sanatorium, I alternated between my perceptions of this weird, unreal, unfamiliar world that I knew was the actual world about me, and visions that presented themselves before me of the world as it was being seen by—by Willard Blackstone.

"My own thoughts were confusing, but sane, absolutely sane, and logically clear. Running along with them, sometimes submerged almost to subconsciousness, at others dominating and subduing the thoughts of my own brain, were the thoughts of Willard Blackstone.

"If you will try and keep in mind, gentlemen, that all this was passing before my eyes and through my brain simultaneously. I can separate it for you, and tell you more intelligently what happened to me."

"Tell us about your wife," suggested the Very Young Man.

"The extraordinary aspect of the real world—the hospital room," went on Jones, staring straight before him, "became less and less confusing as time went on. I realized that after a time I must relearn completely the words that fitted nearly everything I saw, smelled, tasted, heard, and felt. And even the words themselves, the entire language was unfamiliar.

"It was several months, I think, before I was able to make much of a start in this reeducation of my brain. Yet my mentality, internally, so to speak, was always keenly alert. My physical health improved steadily.

"It was four years—four years before I left the sanatorium. I would have been there yet if I had had to entirely readjust my mentality to those new-world impressions. But, after the first year, the—the effect of the other man's blood began very gradually to diminish. This I first noticed just about the time I was beginning to communicate a little with the nurses caring for me.

"Through another most confusing period I found my senses gradually receiving more and more familiar impressions. I became what you—you would call normal about six years ago, and was discharged from the sanatorium. I said very little about myself to the Doctors during my period of recovery. I started to when I first began to talk a little, but I was met with such incredulity, my statements were to them so obviously the result of a disordered brain, that I soon gave up the attempt to explain.

"And so my case has remained unexplained. I returned to normality, although even now I am just a little confused at times. And my friends, what few I have made," he paused and smiled his sad, whimsical smile, "tell me I have—tell me I have sometimes a most annoying habit of repeating my words." He stopped speaking, and looked at the intense faces of those about him.

Silence fell upon the room. The smoke hung heavy about the little group of men stated under the center light. Then the Banker shifted his feet uneasily.

"Tell us the other side of your story," he said gruffly.

"About your wife," said the Very Young Man.

The smile faded from Jones's face. His lips set themselves into a thin, hard line, and again the red spots burned in his cheeks.

"Yes," he said. "I'll tell you the whole story—the whole story as I came to learn it from the thoughts of Willard Blackstone, and from his actions as I saw them with his eyes during the weeks and months I was in the hospital and in the sanatorium. I will—will make it as short as I can. It's a story I—I—

"Willard Blackstone was professor of chemistry at Rexford when I went there. He was a bachelor, a few years older than I. He was a clever chemist, and really more than a clever bacteriologist, with a taste for original research work, although he had distinguished himself in no way.

"He became in time a frequent visitor at our home. My—my wife and I both liked him. He—he fell in love with her almost at once, and it became the dominating desire of his life to get her away from me.

"I don't know just what occurred. You see I only got this part of his blurred memories that passed through my mind. But I know that he tried all the usual ways to win her. And he did it so carefully, so—so diplomatically he never lost her regard, her—her friendship, even though she discouraged him definitely and finally.

"I knew nothing of all this. I liked Willard Blackstone, and I was very much absorbed in my work. My—my wife never said anything to me of it, and so outwardly we all continued to be good friends.

"It was, perhaps, a year after I came to Rexford that Blackstone began seriously to take up his secret study of the human blood. For some time it had been in his thoughts to—to do away with me. Many ways were at his command if he wanted to—to murder. But he was afraid.

"Then came the idea of insanity, and he resolved to do something to me that would make me insane. The more he thought about this, the more picturesque a means of disposing of me it seemed. It became an obsession with him; he worked on the problem into which his researches led him almost constantly.

"I had always been anemic. I suppose it was because of that he came to think of the blood, and the possibility of introducing something into it that would derange the brain. I remember distinctly how one day he made me give him a sample of my blood that he proposed to analyze, and so tell me what was the matter with me."

Jones stopped for a moment. "Gentlemen," he went on, "I suppose you all know more about the blood than I do."

"Maybe he does," said the Very Young Man, indicating the Alienist.

"Maybe," said the Country Doctor, and twinkled over his glasses.

"What I know about the blood wouldn't help us a bit," said the Big Business Man.

"I can't go into technicalities," resumed Jones, "regarding the theories upon which Blackstone based his researches. I know very little about medicine; I have never studied it. I wanted to—afterward, but—it frightens me. All I do know about the blood I got from Blackstone's thoughts. I'll make it as clear as I can. Some of it I don't understand myself.

"As all of you gentlemen know, the blood is a circulating fluid from which the tissue cells extract their nutriment, and into which they discharge the waste products resulting from their activity. To supply nutriment and eliminate waste are the two principal functions of the blood."

"I knew that," said the Very Young Man. "Does it do anything else?"

"Another most important function of the blood," went on Jones, "is seen in the way in which it is employed in protecting the body from disease." He turned toward the Alienist and the Country Doctor, and addressed them almost questioningly, with an obvious deference to their greater knowledge on the subject:

"The blood may fight this invasion of alien living organisms in several ways. It may create some chemical substance to neutralize the toxic material produced by the organism, it may produce a chemical to act as a poison to the organism, thus killing it or rendering it powerless, or the wandering cells of the blood—the leucocytes or white corpuscles—may attack the organism directly and eat it up.

"Do I make it dear?" he asked the Alienist. The Alienist nodded.

6

"HORMONES"

"NOW YOU'RE TALKING sense," said the Banker; "the first intelligent stuff I've heard this evening."

The Big Business Man laughed. "Familiar tunes are sweetest, aren't they, George?" he said.

"Blackstone's first plan," continued Jones, "was to develop some poison that he could introduce into my blood which would have the peculiar power of permanently affecting the cells of the brain, and yet leave the body in normal health. He analyzed my blood carefully, several specimens, I remember he made me give him. It was his idea, I suppose, to find out the weak points and to play upon them.

"I imagine"—he turned to the Alienist again—"that there must be a number of fairly well known chemicals with which he could have accomplished his purpose, at least in part. It was while he was considering this problem, and finding it not at all satisfactory, that an entirely new idea came to him. This was so much more—more picturesque it appealed to him at once. And it seemed to offer no possible risk to himself."

"It was blood transfusion," the Very Young Man burst out.

"Blackstone by this time must have had a tremendous theoretical knowledge of the chemistry of the blood—my blood, and his own in particular, for naturally it was his own blood that offered the greatest opportunity for his study. He had worked with them both so much, it was natural the thought of transfusion should come to him. Then, too, my health suggested a transfusion at this time. That was the important fact that made his new scheme seem to him so feasible.

"You see, when he had decided to poison me directly, however cleverly he might do it, however subtle a poison he might use, there always remained the risk of detection, or at least suspicion, especially in view of his intentions— his intentions subsequently toward my—my wife. That was the reason why he hesitated.

"Now with the plan of a blood transfusion, everything would be different. He knew whatever happened to me then would be attributed to the operation. It afforded a perfect alibi, so to speak, for any harm that might come to me.

"His plan now was to cultivate in his own blood such alien organisms as would be fatal when introduced into mine."

"I should think he would have injured himself," interrupted the Big Business Man.

"Not necessarily," said the Alienist.

"His problem was," went on Jones, "first to find some chemical that when introduced into the blood would produce the effect he desired—permanent destruction of the intelligence—or even—even death he was not adverse to now.

"Another necessary qualification was that this poison must be of such a nature that he could introduce it into his own veins, in small quantities at first, without harm to himself, gradually increasing the quantity as his system became inured to its effects."

"Dope fiends get that way, don't they?" put in the Very Young Man.

"He knew that part of it would be practical," continued Jones, "for, as I have said, he was a remarkably healthy man, and I was—was just the opposite.

"Without much trouble he decided upon his poison, or, rather, some combination of poisons he prepared. The first experiment he made with guinea pigs. One he inoculated over a period of several weeks, then some of its blood he injected into another. The other one died. That seemed to promise success."

"Cheerful sort of villain, this Blackstone," murmured the Playwright.

"If seems to me," said the Country Doctor, "your friend Blackstone was quite a bit of a fool."

The Banker looked across at him with a sarcastic grin. "There's hope," he said, "if somebody will admit something is foolish."

Jones smiled quietly in answer to the Country Doctor's remark. "You anticipate me," he said.

"Blackstone was overlooking one very important fact, and when he thought of it, he was furious at himself for being such a fool. He had got far enough along to have begun inoculating himself, when suddenly it occurred to him that before any physician would accept him for the transfusion operation upon me, his blood would have to be tested. And when that was done, its abnormality would of course be discovered. He had never thought of that before, and when he did it seemed to be an unsurmountable difficulty."

"Gee, that's so," said the Very Young Man, looking blankly around, as though he, too, had encountered an obstacle he could not overcome.

"Even then Blackstone did not give up the idea of blood transfusion, for it seemed to hold possibilities that appealed to—to his sense of the dramatic."

"His persistence was worthy of a better cause," said the Playwright.

Jones smiled again. "He never relaxed his efforts for a moment," he said. "I don't know just what started him on the theories of the difference in individual perception or interpretation by the senses. That's rather a lame way of putting it," Jones interrupted himself apologetically, "but you all know what I mean. I think it was an argument we had one evening. I remember it quite well. We were talking about the difference between sound-waves and sound, that sound-waves were only vibration, and could exist without an ear to hear them. But they were not sound. That only came into being, so to speak, with the existence of an eardrum and a brain to transform the vibrations into what we call sound. We got into quite the same sort of argument you gentlemen were having a while ago.

"To me these theories were only amusing. I forgot them soon after. To Blackstone they opened up a whole realm of possibilities. He studied everything in philosophy on the subject, and, combining that with the knowledge he already had of the blood, finally planned a solution of the problem. This was the plan he ultimately brought to so—so successful a conclusion.

"The basis of Blackstone's theory was that if he could, through blood transfusion, so impress his own individuality upon mine as to make his the dominating force in my brain, my intelligence would be rendered useless. As you all know, that is, in effect, what happened."

"What made him think it would happen in your case?" asked the Playwright. "It never happened in blood transfusion before."

"He didn't expect it to just happen," answered Jones; "he made it happen."

"How'd he do that?" asked the Very Young Man.

"In his study of the anatomy and physiology of the blood," Jones began again, "Blackstone came to believe that somehow in the human blood lay the secret of that indefinable something we call personality—something which marks us as different from each of our fellow mortals—something that makes the blood of each of us unique, different from any other human blood.

"He knew, as all you gentlemen know, that in general structure all human blood is the same. The red corpuscles, white corpuscles, and many other cells whose names I never heard of, may vary very greatly in number in the blood of different people. But in general characteristics their structure is the same. The functions they perform are always the same, and, as you know, they will act the same in the veins of one person as in another. So he knew that in none of them could lie the secret for which he searched."

Jones paused, and then addressed the Alienist directly.

"You have heard of the *hormones?*" he asked. "You know about them?"

"What there is to know," said the Alienist, smiling.

"I never heard of them," said the Very Young Man.

"The *hormones*, as I understand it," continued Jones, "are chemical substances, which are sent through the blood-stream like messengers from one group of tissue cells to excite another group of cells to activity. Not very much is known about then, I guess, and I understand that recently they have been made the subject of considerable research work. They are supposed to play a very important though mysterious part in the diseases attacking the human body. Is that right?" he added to the Alienist.

The Alienist nodded gravely. "The *hormones* are by far the most interesting as well as the least understood cells in the blood. Those of the thyroid gland particularly are now the subject of study."

Blackstone reasoned that possibly some of these *hormones*, especially those acting upon the tissue cells of the brain, might be individual in their functions," continued Jones. "I don't know quite how to explain what I mean. The idea is that whereas the red corpuscles in my blood would act much as the red corpuscles in your blood, some of the *hormones* in mine are individual with me, and in your blood would, under ordinary circumstances, not act at all. This Blackstone believed, and he believed also that it was because these *hormones* would not act upon any other tissue cells than those particular ones for which they were created, that no transfusion of blood had ever carried with it any marked transfusion of the personality of the person giving the blood.

"What Blackstone was able to learn of the *hormones* that was not already known at that time, or that since has been discovered, I cannot say. My impressions were confused, and also I had no way of understanding the complicated technicalities of such impressions as I did get. But I know that he must have discovered a great deal. What he did was to work upon such of these bodies in his own blood—those that were created to act upon the tissue cells of his brain—increasing their power, their—their virility, I suppose you would call it. He also was able to greatly increase their number. It was those specially created *hormones* in his blood that overcame the weaker ones in mine, and so impressed upon my brain his individuality."

"What an idea!" ejaculated the Country Doctor, while the rest of the men stared blankly at each other.

"Everything went off about as Blackstone intended," continued Jones, after a moment of silence during which no one had any question to offer. "You know all about that part of it already."

"Tell us what happened to Blackstone and—and Mrs. Jones," said the Very Young Man eagerly.

"I think I'm hungry," said the Banker. "Crackers and cheese," he suggested with an expansive gesture—"and coffee. Push that button, will you, boy?" The Very Young Man did so, and then helped himself to the Playwright's cigarettes.

Jones sat staring at his feet, apparently undecided how to continue.

"You will remember, gentlemen," he said finally. "I mentioned having seen—having seen them in the railway coach going back to Rexford. That was about three weeks, I think, after the operation.

"My case was soon pronounced hopeless, and, as I have said, I was in due time committed to a sanatorium. Mrs. Jones continued living at Rexford.

"The trustees of Rexford University were very good to her. They—they let her keep our house, and continued my salary for several months.

"Gentlemen, I'm—I'm afraid I shall have to make this part of my story very short. Somehow I—I just can't seem to tell it to you."

The Playwright patted him on the shoulder with a smile, and made him take another cigarette. "You're all right, old man. Go ahead. Sure we understand."

"During this time," began Jones again, "they—they were naturally thrown together very closely, and it was on Blackstone she—she came to depend. Oh, I don't want to excuse her for what happened; but God knows it must have been hard for her those months, and then to—to make up her mind to go—to go away with him.

"They went to Paris first. I could follow them there in the visions; and by what I saw happen and heard, and—and by Blackstone's thoughts, I soon knew their life together was not happy. Then they came here to America, and Blackstone secured a good position with a chemical manufacturer in Chicago.

"It was about this time that the influence of his blood in my veins began to wear off. I began to see the world about me in the sanatorium more clearly. And coincidental with that, the visions of Blackstone's world began to fade. God!

how I struggled to keep them clear, how I fought to try and keep on seeing what—what became of her.

"I soon lost contact with Blackstone's thoughts entirely. Things were pretty bad between him and her at that time. He—he treated her shamefully. Sometimes what I heard him say, and what I saw, almost—almost killed me. And always there was nothing I could do—nothing I could do but just sit and watch—and listen.

"Then one day I could no longer hear them talk—could only see them. And with my eyes open they were gone entirely—the real world was too clear, too strong, and it blotted them out. Only with my eyes closed could I distinguish them—dim, blurred fragments of scenes in their life, everyday getting dimmer, more elusive.

"Then one night I saw them quarrel, and he—he struck her. He struck her, gentlemen—he struck my wife." Jones was sitting up very straight now. His cheeks burned red, and his eyes gleamed with that strange, unearthly light. There was in his voice a new note, almost of exaltation.

"I was sitting alone when—when he struck her. I started to my feet. I think I shouted as I ran forward. I must have hit my head against something, and when I recovered consciousness, the vision was gone. I—I never saw them again."

Jones's voice dropped to its former colorless tone. "That's all I know, gentlemen," he said. "I never saw or heard of them again. And ever since I have been looking for her—and for him. Because—because, you see—I don't know what became of her; I'm just looking—looking for her because—because I don't know where she is." His voice trailed away and died. Drooping down in his chair, he looked very pathetic and utterly ineffective.

7

A SÉANCE OF BLOOD

THE ALIENIST WAS the first to speak after a long pause, during which the men sat smoking in awed silence, each thinking over the amazing things he had heard.

"Extraordinary story," muttered the Alienist. Then crossed over to where Jones, still huddled down in his chair, sat lost in the memories he had aroused.

"You had a terrible experience," he said kindly, putting his hand on Jones's shoulder. Then he sat down on the arm of the chair. "Haven't you ever heard of—them since?" he asked.

"No," said Jones softly. "For years I have been looking— looking everywhere. I have never seen or heard anything of either of them."

"Did you go to Chicago?" asked the Very Young Man.

Jones looked up at him and smiled his slow, weary smile. "I've been everywhere—everywhere possible," he answered. "I have a little income of my own—not very much"—he looked down at his shabby clothes—"but enough."

"What did you find out in Chicago?" persisted the Very Young Man.

"Nothing," answered Jones. "Blackstone and—and she

had left months before I got there. I don't know where they went; I don't even know if—if they were still together."

"You've had a terrible experience," said the Alienist again, and held out his hand. Then he crossed back to his own seat beside the Banker.

"How about that coffee you spoke of?" he asked.

"You're right. Where's that waiter?" roared the Banker, getting up and pushing the bell violently.

"Gee, I'm awfully sorry for you," said the Very Young Man. "I wish we could help. Can't we?"

"I'm afraid I don't see how. But thank you very much; you're all very kind, gentlemen. Your sympathy I—"Jones stopped abruptly, and seemed quite overcome by his emotion.

"Here, waiter," shouted the Banker. "Hurry up! Darn it, this is a rotten club."

"It's a pretty good club," said the Country Doctor.

"You have to like it," said the Alienist, "you're a guest."

"I'm a guest, too," smiled Jones.

"I said it was a rotten club," said the Banker with finality.

The Country Doctor turned toward Jones. "May I ask—" he began. "You seem to have quite recovered your faculties. There have been no ill effects from your experience?"

"I suppose not. No, I don't think so," said Jones. "Only I—I acquired one or two very—very remarkable powers."

"How do you mean?" asked the Very Young Man.

"I didn't find it out until about three years ago," began Jones. "Just as an experiment an acquaintance of mine injected a few drops of his blood into my veins with a hypodermic. I—I found that for a short space of time I could read—could read his thoughts."

"The effect wore off in a few minutes," continued Jones, after a moment's pause. "Yet during that time I got very very distinct thought impressions—more distinct than I ever got from Blackstone even."

"Great Scott!" said the Big Business Man. "That's weird. What could you see?"

"With my eyes open, things were only very slightly disturbed. With them closed, I got vivid pictures of what the other man was thinking about. We tried it several times; it was always the same. Only we found that some thoughts he could hide from me—the ones he resolutely kept in the back of his head. Only those that were uppermost in his mind, so to speak, I could—could read."

"Do you go into a trance?" asked the Very Young Man.

"Oh, no, it's not like that," answered Jones. "You see, I get the other man's thoughts much like pictures floating before me. But I never confuse them with my own. I seem to know the difference always. And I can shut them off when I like by talking about my own thoughts, for instance. No, it's not like a trance; I always have complete possession of my faculties."

"How do you explain your ability to get these thoughts from another person?" asked the Big Business Man.

"I don't know," said Jones thoughtfully, "I've often—often tried to reason it out. My blood must be more susceptible, I suppose."

"I imagine we could explain it theoretically if we thought about it enough," said the Alienist.

"I'll bet you could," said the Banker sarcastically. "You could explain anything if you had time."

"It works," said Jones. "I've tried it with two other people since."

"Try it with us," suggested the Very Young Man eagerly.

"What were the other powers you acquired?" asked the Big Business Man.

"One other," said Jones. "When anyone gives me some of his blood, I seem to be able temporarily to exert an influence over him. I ran make him do as—as I say—if he'll look at me. It's—it's hypnotic, I think."

"Your eyes look funny sometimes," said the Very Young Man.

"I've noticed it," said the Big Business Man; "they do look hypnotic."

"Distance has a good deal to do with it," went on Jones. "I seem to lose my influence unless I am quite close to the person. The thoughts are not so clear, either."

"Try it on us," suggested the Very Young Man again.

The Playwright jumped to his feet excitedly. "Let me manage this," he almost shouted. "By gracious, but this would make a wonderful play."

"Sit down," said the Banker.

"You don't mind, do you?" asked the Very Young Man, appealing to Jones.

"It's rotten bad taste, you know, after what he's been—" began the Big Business Man.

"But it would he awfully interesting, wouldn't it?" put in the Country Doctor slyly.

"I don't mind," assented Jones, "if you really want me to."

"Do we? Oh, gee, it's great," said the Very Young Man, moving his chair back to make more room.

"Come in, Slade," greeted the Alienist, as the clubroom

door opened. The newcomer crossed the room and looked inquiringly at the little group of men by the table.

"Hello, Orrin," said the Playwright. "Meet Mr. Slade, gentlemen," he went on with a flourish: "famous pianist Orrin Slade—you've heard of him. Won't bother with the names, Orrin. All members of this club," he finished grandiloquently.

The Musician bowed with a smile, and drew up a chair among them. He was a distinguished-looking man, dignified and quiet in demeanor. He was dressed in dark clothes, with a high, black stock. His features were large and cast in an irregular mold. He wore his hair slightly longer than average.

"Whatever you're doing, gentlemen, you evidently find it tremendously interesting," he said.

"You bet your life," said the Playwright enthusiastically. "Great stuff—wonderful stuff. Listen, meet Mr. Jones first. He's the main guy here. Mr. Jones—Mr. Slade. Can't tell you much, Orrin, we want to get ahead. Listen." And helped out by the Very Young Man, he told briefly, and quite incoherently, what they were about to do.

"Now, we're all set," he finished. "Let's get this right. This is wonderful stuff. Lock those doors, will you?" The Very Young Man jumped up. "Turn out those side-lights, too," he ordered. "Must do this right."

"Wait a minute; wait a minute," interrupted the Banker. "Let's get the coffee first."

"I'll get it," said the Very Young Man.

"Charge it to me, boy; and get some cigars," said the Banker as the Very Young Man hurried out.

When he came back, the Playwright had shoved the

table over against the wall. The men were seated in a semi-circle across the room, with Jones facing them.

"Get my case, will you?" asked the Country Doctor as the Very Young Man put his tray on the table. "It's in the check-room. Wait, here's the check."

The Very Young Man was back in a moment.

"Now then, we're ready," said the Playwright, putting out all the light except two in the center chandelier. "Lock those doors."

"Why lock the doors?" asked the Banker.

"Mustn't be interrupted," said the Playwright; "besides it's more dramatic."

"When he gets exposing the dark secrets of our lives, some of us may want to get out," laughed the Big Business Man.

"That's the idea. Nothing doing," said the Playwright. "I'm going to run this night. This is great stuff."

The room was now in semi-darkness, with only a circle of light on the rug in the center and the corners quite in the shadow.

"Gee, this is spooky," said the Very Young Man.

"Lock those doors," ordered the Playwright. "Who's that?" he added.

One of the doors had opened, and a man stood hesitating on the threshold. The light from the outer room made him plainly visible—a stalwart figure in the uniform of captain of the English Army.

"Oh, it's Captain Ramsden," said the Country Doctor after a moment of silence. "I met him this afternoon," he added aside to the others. "Can he come in?"

The Playwright stepped forward. "Captain Ramsden,"

he said, and bowed magnificently, "pleased to make your acquaintance, sir. Step right over here, Captain," and he indicated a vacant chair next to the Very Young Man at the side of the room.

"Gentlemen, Captain Ramsden," said the Playwright. "All members of this club, Captain," he finished, and bowed again.

The newcomer looked around him pleasantly and smiled. He was the conventionally handsome type of man, with strong, clean-cut features, and just a hint of unpleasantness about the mouth.

"If I'm not intruding," he said, and seated himself beside the Very Young Man. Then he laughed. "What is it, may I ask—a séance?"

"Worse," said the Banker, "much worse."

"There's nothing worse than a séance," said the Captain.

"Call it anything you like," cried the Playwright. Little play, private theatricals, charade—anything you like. No time to explain now; you'll see."

"Does the food go with it?" asked the Captain. "This tray looks inviting."

"Help yourself," said the Playwright. "Is that door locked?" he added to the Very Young Man. "Wait, never mind, I'll lock it." He locked both doors and dropped the keys in his pocket.

"Now then," he said, coming back to the center of the room; "I guess we're all ready this time. Who's first?"

"Take him," said the Very Young Man, pointing to the Banker.

"Yes, we'll start with you, eh, George?" agreed the Big Business Man.

"No, you won't; not me," said the Banker. "I've got enough trouble."

"Start with me," said the Very Young Man. "How do you get the blood? Does it hurt?"

"I'll decide," said the Playwright. "I'm running this. Who's got a blank sheet of paper."

"Here, said the Very Young Man, handing him part of a letter.

The Playwright tore it into small, square pieces. "How many are we? Eight," he counted, and wrote each name upon a slip of paper.

"Now then, draw," he added, shuffling them up in his hands.

The Very Young Man drew one, and held it in the circle of light. "It's you," he said, indicating the Playwright.

A murmur of applause and laughter rippled across the room. The Playwright looked just a little scared. "How do you get the blood?" he asked.

"Now you are in for it," laughed the Big Business Man. "I'll bet it most kills you."

"Tough luck," sympathized the Banker, and looked pleased for the first time during the evening.

"Rats!" said the Country Doctor, "Where's my case? I'll do it."

In a moment he had his hypodermic out, and the Playwright, looking like a little frightened schoolboy, was having the lobe of his ear cleaned off with a bit of moistened cotton.

"Ouch!" he cried at the sharp prick of a needle in his ear.

When the Country Doctor was ready he motioned Jones to come forward. Jones had been sitting in the semi-darkness. As he rose and walked under the light there came the sharp crack of breaking china from the floor of the room.

"Good God! What's that?" cried the Banker.

"Someone must have dropped a cup." It was the voice of the Big Business Man speaking.

The Very Young Man stooped under one of the chairs, and swept the bits of a shattered coffee cup beneath the table with his hand.

"Give me some more coffee," said the Banker. "This business gets my nerves all on edge."

When Jones had received the injection of blood he seated himself under the light, his figure thrown sharply into prominence. The eight men facing him, outside the circle of light, could only be seen dimly through the gloom.

Several minutes of silence followed, broken only by the heavy breathing of the Banker and the occasional sound of one of the men shifting uneasily in his chair. Jones sat motionless, his face buried in his hands. Then he began to speak slowly, hesitatingly, and softly at first, more rapidly and distinctly as he progressed. His voice was pitched in a monotone as expressionless as one who talks in his sleep.

"Its very dark and dim," he began. "I can't see, the dark is too heavy in between. I see a bridge—a big, high bridge over a river. I can see the lights of the boats passing underneath. Now a street—a street crowded with people. It's a theater letting out. Wait, you go too fast. It's all dim and blurred. I can't see."

8

THE VOICE OF JONES
BUT THE MIND OF–?

JONES STOPPED A moment. His head was still bowed, his hands tightly pressing his forehead. Then he began again; his voice rapidly gathering force.

"Now it's clearer—much clearer. Can't you keep it that way? A bedroom in a hotel. There's a woman in the bed, and a white-capped nurse moving about the room. Beside the woman's bed is a cradle. The woman is speaking now to the nurse, but I can't hear her, I'm too far away.

"The nurse picks up the baby and lays it beside the mother. Now she goes out into the adjoining room. It's clearer now; that's good. A man enters the room; he is dressed in business clothes. He puts his overcoat and hat in the closet. I can't see him very well. He keeps his face turned away. He kisses the woman. Now he is sitting by the bedside looking at the baby. The man and woman are talking. I can hear them a little; I can't make out what they are saying."

Jones's voice rose suddenly to a higher pitch.

"Think of what they're saying," he commanded, raising his head. "I can't—I want to know what they're saying." Then he bowed his head again and his voice dropped to its monotone.

"That's better. The man is angry. Now the woman is crying a little. But I can't hear—

"Now the man is pacing up and down the room. He stops by the bed to speak again to the woman. I can't see his face. The features are blurred.

"The woman is clearer; yes; now I can see her plainly. She is pretty—very pretty, but very wan and pale. Now the man gets his hat and overcoat. Now he goes out and slams the door.

"A big building—it looks like a factory. I can see the street lights. The building is dark; there are no lights in its windows. The street is deserted; it is late evening. The houses here are small—the homes of poor people. A man comes up the street. He stops at the door of the factory. He has a key, he lets himself in. Who is he? I can't see his face. Who is he?" Jones's voice again rose to its commanding tone. Then he relaxed in his chair.

"Oh, the same man. That's better; I see him now. He goes up several flights of stairs. Now he enters an office. It's dark, and he lights a small desk light. A safe in the corner—yes, that is a safe. He opens it easily. He is taking something out and stuffing it in his pocket. I can see it now; it's money—a package of bills.

"There are too many streets—they're all confused. Where is the man? There, that's better—the factory again. The man is coming downstairs. What kind of a factory is it? I can't see. The rooms are all so dark. Yes, I know, a factory where they make chemical instruments. I can see now a great, long shelf—hundreds of little test-tubes."

Someone of the men facing Jones in the gloom pushed his chair back suddenly. The movement made a sharp rasp of sound.

"A chemical factory!" came in a whisper from the Very Young Man.

"Too many streets," went on Jones's voice, unheeding. "They're all confused. Think clearer. There, that's better.

"Is this a theater dressing-room? You'll have to think it clearer. Yes, I see a girl, sitting before a dressing-table rubbing off her make-up. The same man is here now. He kissed her. They are talking. I can almost hear what they are saying. But I'm too far away; I must get up closer."

Jones sat up suddenly very straight. "Come nearer; can't you come nearer?" he said. "I want to hear them talk."

"He tells you to move up closer," whispered the Big Business Man, nudging the Playwright.

Jones was talking again. "I can almost hear them. They are so clear. Come closer."

The Playwright awkwardly hitched his chair forward a few feet.

"Oh, now they're all blurred. Think them clearer. Now, that's better; much better. He says: 'We must go tonight. I've got the money. It's tonight or never. Will you, dear?' The girl nods her head. Oh, now you've let them fade. I only see—

"Now we're at the stage door outside. There's the man waiting with a taxi. The girl comes out. She has a suitcase; they get into the taxi and drive away.

"You must make it clear. I can't see so many streets. One street they're driving down? Yes, now I can see the lights and the people. What city is this? Think the city; I must know the city. Oh, Chicago? Yes, I can tell now it's Chicago.

"A railway station, and they're getting out of the taxi. I see the train; yes, I see the sleeper. They're coming into the car. This is their drawing-room. Where are they going? Yes, now I know; they're going to New York." Jones rose and stepped back a pace from under the light. "Can you wait a moment?" he asked. "I'm tired. I'd like to wait a moment. Think of me, and the room here; just a moment."

The silence that followed was oppressive. After a time Jones sat down again in his chair under the light. "Look at me now," he ordered, staring at the Playwright. "Now—go on—'A week later.' Why have you written it? I can see it in great letters in front of me. Now the letters are fading; I see the hotel room again.

"The woman is still in bed; the baby lies in its cradle. Is the woman asleep? No, I see her eyes are open. What is she thinking? You'll have to think her thoughts clearer. Yes, now I understand. The man has deserted her. She is waiting, but he never comes. Who is the man? Can't you let me know who the man is? The father of her child? Yes, I know that. Not her husband? Has she a husband?

"'A month later.' You've written it again. Why do you write so big? There, now I see the bedroom. The woman is up now; she is sitting in the corner, crying. There is a man sitting beside the cradle. Yes, I see a doctor. The baby is dead. The Doctor rises and stands beside the mother. Now, it's dark—all dark.

"The bedroom again. The woman is packing her clothes. There is no one else in the room. What is she thinking? Yes, now I understand. She is alone in America. Isn't she an American? Oh, English. Yes, I understand. She is going East—to New York—to look for the man who has deserted her. She is sure he went there. And she has some money— not much, but enough for that. And she hopes, perhaps later, to get to England. Yes, I understand. When is she going? Wait—now it's dark.

"This is New York. I see the woman, coming along this street. She goes into a brown-stone house. I know, it's a boarding house. She is going to live there. Then she will go out to find work. What kind of work? Oh, she doesn't know; she has no business training at all. She is in her room now—bare and gloomy, but comfortable.

"Wait—it's fading.

"Oh, the factory office in Chicago, Yes, I see it—plainly now. A stranger enters and makes inquiries. I can't see him clearly. Oh—it's *I*. You're thinking of me? Why are you thinking of me? That is not the right office—but you're thinking of me. What am I asking the factory people? Where the man went? And the woman? Who was the man? I couldn't tell before. You couldn't let me know. I asked you."

Jones's voice had risen excitedly as he poured out these questions. A new note of anger crept into it—and a note of command and authority. He pushed his chair backward violently, rising to his feet.

"What do you know of all this?" he demanded. "You can't hide it from me any longer." He flung his arms out before him. "Look at me—look at me, I say. Now, think. I tell you to think. Who was that other man? Who was he? You can't hide his name from me. You can't, I say. Blackstone! Oh, then it was Blackstone. And the woman he deserted? My—my—"

9

"A MASTERPIECE, GENTLEMEN!"

JONES STOPPED SUDDENLY and took a step backward, "Yes, I know now whom you mean." He was forcing himself to calmness. "But you, who are you that you can know all this? What *do* you know?"

There was an abrupt silence. Then Jones sat down in his chair suddenly and laughed.

"Oh, of course. I never thought of that. Very clever. Naturally, I supposed—"

There came another pause. Then Jones's voice became tense again.

"What do you mean? When? Yes, I'll be careful. But when? I thought I did, but you didn't know it. Oh, you did? You were watching me? And watching him? Yes, more careful. Yes, go on. I'll do my part, of course. Try it."

The Playwright coughed a little, and then cleared his throat violently. In the silence of the room the voice was startling. There followed a breathless pause. Then a match was lighted, disclosing the tense, white face of the Big Business Man as he held it to his cigar.

"God!" said the Banker. "Don't do that." The Big Business Man snuffed out the light.

Jones's voice had begun again. "Can't you think back to

Chicago? Think—yes, in New York. The woman is look-ing for a job. Yes. I see her turned away place after place."

"Now she has a job? Oh, yes, I see the rehearsal chorus girl, a musical show on Broadway.

"Wait; you go too fast. I can't see this man. I see the room. Oh, yes. I see it is a studio—a man's workshop. Yes, I know it is in Greenwich Village. The woman is here. I see her now clearly. It is the same girl. Prettier than she was, but older—much older. And—and just a little coarser.

"There is a man here. Who is he? An author—a play-wright? Now I see him. It looks like *you*. Of course—yes, I see the man now. It looks like you. The woman and he are fast friends? Yes, I know that. He is in love with her—he wants to marry her. He is telling her now—that's it. That is what he is saying.

"He doesn't know her story. She hasn't told him yet. She wonders if she ought to tell him now.

"Wait—now it's all blurred and faded. Yes, I under-stand; she didn't tell him, and she asked him to wait for her answer.

"Now it's gone again. Only a street whirling past. I know, in an automobile. Two men. The Playwright—yes, and—and Blackstone. It *is* Blackstone, only that's not his name now. What *is* his name now? You must know."

"You won't think his name. He looks different now—much different. Yes, I understand—I'd never recognize him, but I know this is Blackstone. He is a friend of the Playwright now? Yes, I know that, too. What is his busi-ness? A professional man—a scientist? Not a chemist? No, I know that. Is he a business man? Oh, you won't tell me—"

"Gentlemen, I—I—" It was the Alienist.

"Sh!" came from the Very Young Man.

"The Playwright's studio again. There is a lot of people in it now. Yes, of course, friends of the Playwright—a studio party. I see the Playwright, sitting apart, talking with his friend Blackstone. I'll have to call him Blackstone, if you won't let me know what his name is now. I can't hear what they are saying. We're too far away. Can't we get up closer?

"He is telling Blackstone about a girl he is very fond of. He wants to introduce Blackstone to her. It is the same girl—yes, I know that. Is she here at the party? She is coming; the Playwright is expecting her any moment.

"Now she comes in. Yes. I see it is the same girl. How pretty she looks. Everyone here knows her. They greet her with shouts. She has made herself a favorite.

"Now she is standing by the Playwright. He puts his hand on her shoulder. I see him turn to introduce her to Blackstone. Oh, they recognize each other. There is a pause—it is an awkward moment, and dramatic. Yes, of course, I see it's dramatic.

"The Playwright doesn't notice anything wrong. His attention is distracted by someone else. He turns away. Blackstone and the girl shake hands casually. They are exchanging swift words in an undertone. Now they are moving apart, joining the others. Wait, you're letting it fade.

"I see the girl at home next evening. Someone phones her—yes, I know, it's Blackstone phoning; I can see him at the other end of the wire. They are arranging a meeting. Yes, I hear them. Now they are in a restaurant. I can't hear them talk—the music makes so much noise. Blackstone is angry. He admits running away with the other girl. What happened to her? You never told us what happened to her. Oh, he has deserted her since?

"The girl sitting at the table with him now is strangely silent. She is thinking hard. What are her thoughts? We ought to know her thoughts, too. Yes, I see. She is thinking she should forget Blackstone and marry the Playwright. She wants to—she knows she ought to tell him everything and marry him if he will have her. But she cannot, for now—he knows she still loves Blackstone—will always love him. That's too bad—too bad.

"She tells Blackstone she loves him, she wants to come back to him. He laughs. Yes, I can hear her pleading—very humble, without pride, even without self-respect. It's too bad, very bad. And he laughs, and the things he says, and what he calls her— She has turned at last.

"Her cheeks are very red—her eyes are flashing. She asks him to take her out and leave her on the street outside. They are getting up to go now.

"The street is crowded with pleasure-seekers. Blackstone and the girl come out, and at the door they part. There is no good-bye; he just leaves her standing there and walks away. She hesitates a moment; she is wondering. Now on an impulse she turns quickly and follows him.

"I see a more quiet street—hotels along here. Blackstone has turned the corner. He is walking fast; he comes closer. I don't see the girl. Yes, now I see her—just a little way behind. Blackstone turns into a broad doorway. What building is it? What? Of course—how stupid! I might have recognized it—*this* building—of course: the Scientific Club!

"Blackstone has gone inside now. The girl stops at the

door, undecided. She is thinking whether she dare follow him in. She is going to wait for him outside. Yes, I see she crosses the street.

"An hour passes. The girl is still waiting. When did this happen? Lately? Oh, only last night. There's Blackstone coming out of the doorway. The girl stops him. They are talking—standing over there in the shadow. We must get up closer; I can't hear. Yes, she is pleading with him again— and threatening. Now I hear her. And he says, "Go to hell!"

"Wait, you've let it slip—it's all confused. What did they do? Oh, yes, he called a taxi and left her standing there. And now she is walking away.

"This afternoon! It's this afternoon you are thinking. I see a little—not very much. It's very dark—there, that's better. But not as clear as it was—nothing's as clear as it was. You must come closer—come closer, don't you understand? You're too far away."

The Playwright slid his chair forward a little. He was just outside the circle of light now, with only a few feet separating him from Jones. The line of chairs in which the other men sat stretched across the darkened room behind him.

"That's better," Jones went on in his dreary monotone. "It's clearer now. This afternoon you're thinking of what happened this afternoon. In the Playwright's studio—of course I know. Your studio, yes, I see it now. I see you both clearly. She is telling you the story of her past life—yes, I hear her. And you still love her. You still want her to marry you. You say that to her. She is crying now. Yes, I know— very, very pathetic.

"She tells you she loves Blackstone—she cannot help loving Blackstone. And she wants to see him again. She has decided she must see him again—tonight. You advise her not to—you try to make her see she must forget him. There is nothing you can do to help her—no, nothing.

"But she insists she must see him. She gets up to go. What did she tell you she was going to do? You are asking her now? And she won't tell you. She looks so pale and tearful—and yet determined. You are afraid of what you might do. And now she goes out, and you sit there alone—thinking.

"She will probably try to see Blackstone tonight. At the club. Of course, she doesn't know where else to find him. You are afraid of what she may do? Yes, I know you must still pretend to be Blackstone's friend. You will meet Blackstone tonight at the club?

"Now I see the inside of the club. What time is this? Tonight, after dinner? I see you now and Blackstone coming in together. The other men join you. Who are they—I see their faces, but there are no features.

"Why are there no features? The men look familiar. I'm sure I know them. Who are they? You must let me understand. Yes, I see a fifth man joining you. Now you are all coming into this room. Yes, I see. Two other men are in the room. One of them is sitting near the center, reading. I've seen him before. Who is he? His face is blurred, too—all the faces are blurred—only Blackstone and you are clear. The five men all seem to know this other man. Yes—I see him greet them. There is still another man in the room, over there in the corner, dozing. *He's* clear—I see his face clearly. It's *I.* Yes, of course. I remember, I was there after supper.

"Now the six men are having an earnest discussion. I know. Theories of size and shape and taste. Yes, I see some of them looking at the moon through the window. None of the men see me sitting there in the corner. They are too much interested in their argument. Oh, now I am making myself known—I begin my story. Of course I remember—it was hardly an hour ago."

Jones paused a moment.

"I'm very tired," he began again, "and my head hurts. It's getting fainter, too—much fainter, much harder to know what you think."

"Gentlemen, I—I must protest—" the Alienist broke in.

"Sh!" came another voice. "Let him finish."

"It's so blurred," continued Jones softly. "Can't you think harder? Yes, I know—it is wearing off. You'll hurry? Yes—all right. Now I see the girl at home. Only an hour ago. She is coming up to the club here to see Blackstone. She will try to force her way into the club. She is desperate. Yes, I see her starting. What time is it now? Oh, just a few minutes ago, probably.

"A taxi coming up Broadway, and the girl inside. Yes, I know she is there, though I cannot see her—it's too faint. This room again. We are still sitting in the same places. What time is this? *Now!* Oh, it's now you are thinking about!"

Jones's voice rose in pitch, and he began talking much faster, almost excitedly it seemed, in contrast to his former measured slowness.

"*Now*, of this very moment, you are thinking! Where is the taxi now? I can't see it.

"I see it, turning in, right here at the corner. She will be here in a moment. This room again. We are all sitting here. No one has moved. How do you know? I can't see anything.

No, nothing. No, I cannot hear anything. Nothing moving. *Somebody moving behind you?* Where? Where?"

A heavy thump resounded through the room, followed by a brief instant of stillness.

The Banker had risen violently from his leather easy-chair and overturned it on the floor behind him.

"Stop!" he cried in a strained voice. "Good God, gentlemen, stop!" He looked around wildly. The others were all seated as before. Apparently no one had moved.

"How can you go on? Which of us is this Blackstone, since he is here? We must find out. You know." He clutched at the Playwright's arm.

"And the girl," he went on excitedly. "She will be here any minute. She may be outside now. I—"

The Playwright tore himself from the Banker's grasp, bounding to his feet. He shoved the Banker back abruptly and stepped under the light.

Not one of the other men moved, but each gripped his chair expectantly. Jones sat quiet, his head in his hands, his figure drooping.

The Playwright stood beside him under the light. The expression on his face was extraordinary.

"Gentlemen," he began with a bombastic gesture, "you have had the privilege of reading my innermost, my secret thoughts. An interesting experiment—a magnificent experiment—complete success."

"But, good Heavens—" began the Banker.

The Playwright raised his hand commandingly.

"What you have heard—dramatic. You must admit it. And thrilling? Terribly thrilling. How does it end? Who knows? Perhaps we will find out if we wait. For it's true to life—very. Perhaps it *is* true—who shall say? A master-piece, gentlemen," and he laughed. "My masterpiece—the basic plot of what the world will someday call the greatest movie ever written!"

10

RETRIBUTION IN BLOOD

IF THE PLAYWRIGHT wished to astound his audience, he certainly accomplished his desire. His words were so utterly unexpected that for a moment no one quite grasped their meaning. The mimic drama he had so deftly unfolded for them had become so real when they found they were actors in it they could not at first credit this statement of its unreality.

Then Jones looked up with his slow, tired smile that confirmed the self-satisfied grin on the Playwright's face.

"Well, I'll be damned!" ejaculated the Banker, and looked around helplessly for a chair.

The Very Young Man jumped up and righted the one he had overturned. The Banker collapsed into it, utterly overcome. For several minutes the men gave vent to their astonishment, while the Playwright stood under the light, grinning at them complacently, and Jones drooped in his chair, his hands over his face.

Then the Banker seemed suddenly to come to himself.

"Switch on those lights!" he exclaimed. "Let's get out of this damnable darkness. Open that window—there's no air in here, I'm stifling."

The Very Young Man hastened to obey, but the Playwright stopped him.

"No, you don't—sit down!" he commanded. "I'm still bossing this thing. I'm not through with you yet."

"Oh, my gosh!" said the Very Young Man, and sat down again.

"Now, then, you listen to me," began the Playwright in a domineering tone. "You gave me leave to start these experiments. Believe me, they're interesting, and I'm going right ahead with my ideas."

"You've got too many ideas—that's the trouble," growled the Banker.

"What do you think you're going to do next?" asked the Big Business Man. For once he did not laugh, and there was just a little note of anger in his voice.

"We're going to try that experiment all over again—with somebody else," answered the Playwright blandly. "That is if Mr. Jones is willing. Are you?" he added.

"Yes," said Jones softly, without looking up.

"Well, I'm not willing," said the Big Business Man shortly.

"Gentlemen, I must protest against any more of this," began the Alienist. "You—"

"You'll kill the little man," added the Country Doctor.

"Will you do it, Jones?" persisted the Playwright.

"Yes," said Jones. "I'm all right."

The bantering smile faded from the Playwright's face.

"Very well, then," he said with finality, "we'll do it. Whom do we take?"

"You'll leave me out," said the Big Business Man.

"Me, too," said the Captain.

"And me," added the Musician.

"I say—"began the Captain; "you know this is—"

"Go 'way from here," growled the Banker, as the Playwright took a step toward him. "For a million dollars I wouldn't have anything to do with you."

The Playwright looked around with a withering scorn.

"Well, you're a fine bunch, I must say! It's lucky I've got these doors locked"—he jingled the keys in his pocket—"or you'd be falling all over yourselves to get away. You might try the window," he added sarcastically; "we're only up about a hundred feet."

No one had any reply to make to this, and the Playwright went on briskly: "We'll draw lots again. Where are those papers? Thank you," he added as the Very Young Man gathered them up and handed them to him.

"Now, then," he continued, shaking up the small squares of paper in his hands after discarding the one that bore his own name. "Say, what are you afraid of, anyway? You've only one chance in seven of being drawn, you know."

The Very Young Man stood ready to draw, when the Alienist interrupted them again.

"It's very unwise," he said. "Look at him," and he pointed to Jones, who still sat huddled in his chair, apparently paying no attention to what was going on around him.

"He's all right," said the Playwright, laying his hand on Jones's shoulder.

At the touch Jones started to his feet. "I said I was all right. I'll do it!" he exclaimed.

Then he sat down again and relapsed into his former attitude.

The Banker slid lower into his chair with his legs stretched out before him, seemingly resigned to his fate.

"Hand me those cigars when you finish that, will you, boy?" he asked the Very Young Man. "Good Lord! how did I ever get into this?" he added with a groan.

The Very Young Man, as before, drew one of the bits of paper and held it under the light.

"Well, speak up, son—who is it?" asked the Playwright impatiently; for the Very Young Man stood silent, staring at the little piece of paper in his hand.

"It's me," he said finally. His face was a study.

"Thank the Lord!" murmured the Banker, with a sigh of relief.

The Playwright hesitated and looked down at Jones. Their glances met; then Jones closed his eyes again, passing his hand over his forehead wearily.

"Oh, well, if it has to be," said the Country Doctor. "Where's my case?"

The Playwright made his decision.

"Wait a moment," he said. "I've another idea."

"Damn your ideas!" muttered the Banker.

"We won't take you," said the Playwright to the Very Young Man.

The Very Young Man looked both relieved and disappointed.

"What do you mean, you won't take him?" asked the Big Business Man.

"No, son, we won't take you," the Playwright repeated.

"Why not?" asked the Very Young Man.

The Playwright assumed again his bantering manner.

"Don't you realize," he asked, "this thing takes class—

real intellect? You saw *me* do it. Classy stuff—concentration, real intellect, that is. No, we won't take you."

"Oh, I say now—"began the Very Young Man.

"Sit down over there," said the Playwright, indicating the Very Young Man's chair.

"Now, then, gentlemen," he continued in his most irritating manner, "I'm running this. Here's my idea."

"Give me that cigar, will you, boy?" said the Banker. "This man's driving me crazy."

"What we ought to do," said the Playwright, "is take each one in turn, till we've had everybody."

"You're a fool," said the Banker. "We'd be here all night."

"And the little man would be dead," added the Country Doctor.

"My idea is," said the Playwright, "since we haven't time to take each one in turn, we'll take 'em all at once."

"Is that what you call an idea?" muttered the Banker. "Great Heavens, what will the man suggest next?"

"It's more than an idea—it's a conception," went on the Playwright grandly. "A wonderful conception—a magnificent conception; a conception worthy even of a greater brain than mine. How about it, Jones?"

"Take them all at once," said Jones, without looking up. "Take them all at once. Yes, I'll try it."

The Playwright bowed. "There you are, gentlemen—he'll try. With simple eloquence he says. 'I'll try.' He'll take them all at once. A most awe-inspiring experiment, gentlemen—a fitting climax to an interesting evening."

"You're a damn fool!" growled the Banker.

"Thank you very much," smiled the Playwright, unruffled. "You think to wound me. Yet gladly will I mix my blood with yours in the veins of this, our mutual friend."

"Your blood," said the Banker. "We had yours once. That's enough."

"I said my blood," said the Playwright, with finality, "and my blood goes."

Then for a moment his manner changed. "Oh, gentlemen, gentlemen," he cried appealingly, "haven't you any sporting instinct? Don't you want to see this thing through to the limit? He's all right," waving his hand toward Jones; "it won't hurt him. Besides," he added shrewdly, "maybe it won't work with us all. Who knows?"

"Where's my case?" said the Country Doctor. "Only— I'm not responsible for this."

"That's the talk. You've got the right idea," laughed the Playwright. "Here's one sport, anyway. Line up, gentlemen."

Helped by the Very Young Man and the Alienist, it took the Country Doctor only a few minutes to draw a few drops of blood from each of the men.

"Right ear this time," said the Playwright when it came his turn. "Same blood, you know—the other ear's sore."

They mixed the blood on a bit of glass, and in a moment more it was injected into Jones, who never moved from his place during the whole proceeding.

When they were quite finished the Playwright heaved a sigh and sat down abruptly. "Back to your places, gentlemen," he said, "and silence."

The men seated themselves as before, only this time the Playwright was much closer to Jones. The room became quite silent.

It was a long time before Jones began to speak. When he did, his voice was so low at first they could hardly hear him.

"Too much—too much," he began. "All dim and blurred and intermingled. Very confusing—almost unintelligible. Yes, *you* I understand. Dominating now, of course. Almost as clear as before. Yes, you're really sure now? Why? Oh! No, I didn't. I was afraid to look.

"Wait. I see the inside of a big building, crowded with people—very dim, but clear now. It's a theatre—no, a concert-hall. Yes, I see a pianist on the stage. Oh, it's *you.* Yes, I recognize you. There's somebody playing billiards— yes, I see you standing by the table; and the table is hanging in mid-air, in that great auditorium. Wait; now there is a— now there are others—oh, so many others, all crowding in.

"Soldiers marching—yes, there, a whole ship-load of them, leaving port. They are crowding the rails, waving. And the Stock Exchange; and there's—there's a hospital. Yes, I see it—a studio, with canvases around. Oh, yes, *you.* Go on—now's the time; hurry. Yes, I understand—I've had him once, faintly, very faintly—but clear. Yes, I know— careful. I will. Now—back—yes. I understand—back— farther away—away—"

The silence of the room was suddenly broken by the rasping sound of a chair sliding on the floor. It was the Playwright shoving his chair back in line with the others.

Jones's voice was continuing: "All dark—so dark. What are you all thinking of? It's fading. What is the matter? It's fading—dark—all dark—all dark."

Jones's voice trailed away into silence and he stopped.

For what seemed an interminable time there was absolute stillness in the room. It was broken by the voice of the Big Business Man.

"Enough of this. It's foolishness now," he said.

"Sh!" faintly whispered the Very Young Man.

"Dark—all dark and blank," went on Jones unheeding. "Yes, go on. Yes, you did notice? Just now. No, I cannot see from here—you're *sure* now? Oh! Yes, I got a little of his real thoughts—just a little—a moment ago.

"Dark—all dark. Where is the street? Only a little street I see, and an automobile. Yes, I'm pretty sure, too. I think I'll do it now—*now*—"

There was a brief pause. Then Jones bounded to his feet and, picking up his chair, flung it behind him across the room with a crash.

"I've got you now!" he fairly shouted. "I've got you now, just where I want you—at last—at last!"

The change in his manner was complete. He stood under the light, his figure drawn to its full height. His cheeks flushed, his eyes flashed fire. His whole demeanor was dominating, forceful, and confident.

"I've got you," he went on. "You can't get away. I've got you, body and soul. You're clever, oh, yes, very clever. But you're not superhuman. You can't control all your thoughts. And now I've got your blood in my veins—your blood in my veins again after all these years."

There was confusion in the room as the men rose in their chairs.

"Switch on those lights, boy!" shouted the Playwright. "Hurry! Not these—over there—all of them. I'll do these."

The room was suddenly flooded with the dazzling light, and for a moment the men stood blinded.

"Back—farther back, all of you!" cried Jones.

They retreated slowly before his advance, fascinated by the power of his flashing eyes.

As he came toward them Jones kicked the chairs aside, clearing a space in front of the men who were now backed almost to the wall of the room.

"I've got him, gentlemen—got him right here, with his blood in my veins, his thoughts in my head. We've been playing a little comedy, gentlemen; but this is real—real at last."

"My God!" began the Banker, "I—I—"

"Silence!" commanded Jones. "Listen to me, all of you. I thought I recognized him when I first saw him tonight. But he's changed, and it was so fantastic an idea—so wild a chance—I thought it just a curious likeness. But *he* saw something later I did not see."

Jones flung out his arm toward the Playwright.

"He suspected and he watched, from his seat in the dark. *I* could not see—I was in the light. And what he saw confirmed his suspicions.

"Then he told me—through his blood. And we played out a little comedy, thinking to trap him. Oh, he's clever, very clever, and he kept quiet. But he's not clever enough, for he gave himself away.

"I know I could have confronted him at once when I was sure. But I wanted his blood in my veins—I wanted his thoughts in my brain. And I've got them, gentlemen—got them now. He can't hide anything from me now."

"Watch him," cautioned the Playwright.

"I'm watching him; I've got him now. But his thoughts are blurred and confusing."

Jones flashed his glance back and forth across the line of men.

"Look at me, all of you." He took a step forward. "Look at me—look at my eyes—my eyes, I tell you." He met the eyes of each in turn. "Think of me," he commanded. "Think only of me—there, that's better. All the same thoughts now. Keep it that way. Keep it that way, I say."

"Closer to him," said the Playwright; "then you'll get it."

Jones turned suddenly to the side. "I'm getting it clearer now. You can't stop thinking. It's superhuman—you can't stop thinking. Where is she? What became of her? That's what I must know. You've got to think of it. You can't hide it from me now."

He strode forward and confronted one of the men, who stood with his back against the wall, near the side of the room.

"Look at me, I say—you can't avoid my eyes that way. That's it—you must. Now think. What did you do with her? Where is she? Oh, I—"

Jones's body wavered and he put his hand to his eyes.

The Playwright started forward, but Jones recovered himself in an instant.

"I'm all right. I—I couldn't realize—" His voice broke.

"So she's dead," he went on in a lower tone. Then his anger suddenly broke forth. He flung his arms out before him, and one of them brushed the man's shoulder. Then man shrank from the touch. "Are you thinking the truth? Is it true? When did she die, and how—how? You must think—I command you to think how she died. A suicide! She killed herself! You drove her to it. You—you miserable—"

"Look out!" shouted the Very Young Man shrilly. "He's got a gun!"

The man's hand was slowly moving to his side.

"I know you're armed," said Jones. The suppressed passion in his tense tones thrilled his hearers. "I know you've got a gun—yes—a little one there in your pocket. But you can't get your hand to it. Her revolver! The very one she killed herself with! That's what you are thinking!"

Jones abruptly broke into weird, eerie laughter.

"The revolver she killed herself with! Retribution, gentlemen." He brought his hand down heavily upon the man's shoulder. Then he stopped backward a few paces.

"Stand aside, gentlemen," he cried, waving his arms. "Out of the way, all of you. Retribution—at last!"

The other men drew to the side at Jones's command, leaving him facing his enemy. For an instant the two men eyed each other in silence.

Then Jones spoke again. "I've got you now—got you, body and soul. And you're afraid—afraid of me—little Jones!" and again he laughed.

"Take out the revolver!" he commanded. "Take it out, I say. Is it loaded? Is it? Oh, it is! Now, that's it—you have it in your hand now. Bring it out—bring it out, I say. There, now, raise it up. No, not this way—at yourself, of course, at yourself. Not your heart—no, your temple. Up with it—up with it, I say. Press it hard—there, that's it. Press it hard. Is your finger on the trigger? Now—*fire!*"

A shot rang through the room; the body of Captain Ramsden hung wavering an instant, and crashed to the floor.

THE THOUGHT-GIRL

1

IN THE WEST forties of New York, not far from Fifth
Avenue, stands the huge building that houses the Scientific
Club. It is a full block in depth, and fifteen stories high.
Two great columns flank its northern entrance, and on its
broad flat roof is a garden of shrubs and flowers, with little,
winding white-graveled paths, and pergolas trellised with
roses and with honeysuckle.

One small corner of the garden is roofed over. Underneath is a polished hardwood floor, carpeted with mats of
straw. There are a number of large wicker chairs, several
small tables, and one very large circular table of wicker
near the center. From the roof, over this table, depends a
huge electrolier, casting its yellow beam almost directly
downward.

On rainy evenings, sliding panels of glass make this
enclosure a room where, if you can be alone, you will find a
solitude awesome and uncanny. When the weather is clear
these panels are rolled back. Then you can hear vague and
confused strains of music wafted up from the restaurant
on the floor below; you seem to be sitting, then, upon a
windswept veranda, luxuriously cool, at peace with yourself and with the world.

On such an evening as this, in the latter part of August,
a little group of men, members of the club most of them,

were sitting in this enclosure talking earnestly. On one
of the smaller tables, with two empty chairs beside it, a
chessboard with its red and white figures lying meaning-
lessly about, showed where a game had been forsaken. All
the men in the room were gathered now around the larger
table.

The garden beside them, unlighted except by the stars
and the moon, whispered with the hushed voices of its
occupants. It was Sunday—the one night when women
were allowed to come up from the city below. The softness
of their voices, and sometimes the silvery ripple of their
laughter, mingled with the music that filled the air. But
they laughed seldom, for here in this garden under the sky,
one did not often feel like laughing.

Around the wicker table, in the yellow glow of light from
above, the magic spell of the night outside was broken.
The black-coated men gathered there paid no heed to the
stars, or to the moon. They did not even hear the music
that floated in to them. They laughed, they frowned; they
spoke heatedly, jokingly, or with anger, as one does in the
world of realities. Only somehow, they always seemed to
speak softly, as though subconsciously they desired not to
intrude their voices upon the solemn quiet of the garden
so near them.

One of the men, he around whom the conversation
seemed to center, was a well-known professor of one of
the Middle-western universities. He had belonged to the
club for many years, and had scores of friends among its
members, although he visited New York infrequently. He
sat now leaning back at ease in his chair with his elbows

upon its broad arms and his feet stretched out upon its extended foot rest, as one reclines in a chair on shipboard.

"You ask me rather a difficult question, gentlemen," he said thoughtfully.

"I can answer it," burst out the Very Young Man. "Thought is the result of the act of thinking."

"Many more profound minds than ours have puzzled over that question," put in the Doctor, ignoring the Very Young Man, and addressing the Professor directly.

"I am not a metaphysician," said the Professor, looking around at the interested faces of his companions. "My conception of thought is rather more from the scientific than the philosophical viewpoint."

"Just what do you mean by scientific?" asked the Big Business Man.

The Professor considered a moment.

"I think I can explain it best by giving you an analogous case," he said. "Music, for instance, is generally considered one of the arts, rather than a science. We discuss music almost entirely from the artistic viewpoint; we judge it by artistic standards. Yet it has its scientific aspect as well. It is, if you think of it that way, merely a matter of vibration. The timbre of a violin differs from that of a piano only in the variety of its wavelengths; one note differs from another only in its rate of vibration. That, we may say, is the scientific side of music. So it is with thought as I conceive it."

"You mean thought has something to do with vibration?" suggested the Big Business Man.

"Thought *is* vibration," said the Professor quietly. "Simply that. Nothing more or less in its physical sense, than inaudible vibration."

"Gosh," ejaculated the Very Young Man, incredulously. "I never knew thought was physical; I always believed it was mental."

"That will lead us into metaphysics again," said the Professor smiling.

"Almost everything is vibration, isn't it, if you come to that?" put in the Big Business Man. "Sound is, of course; and light, and heat."

"And the telephone," added the Very Young Man, "and X-rays, and wireless—"

The Professor smiled again. He had a way of smiling that suggested a far greater knowledge of his subject than any of his companions; yet there was in his smile no trace of patronage.

"I believe you are right," he said thoughtfully. "Vibration is one of the most universal attributes of matter. Audible vibrations, we call sound. You have mentioned several other forms of vibration that produce phenomena recognized by our senses. But the most fundamental of all is molecular vibration—the vibration of molecules of matter. Without that, our universe as we know it, would cease to exist."

"Vibration itself is not matter, is it?" asked the Big Business Man.

"No, it is merely a movement of matter," the Professor replied, "one of its most fundamental attributes. Incidentally, just between you and me, I believe it is a subject very incompletely understood by modern physicists."

"What makes you say thought is vibration?" asked the Banker suddenly, opening his eyes and sitting up in his chair. Evidently he had been listening to the conversation intently, although by his look he might have been drowsing.

"I have proven it conclusively many times," the Professor answered. "But I did not originate the idea—do not think that. Professor Flournoy, Sir William Crookes, and many others have agreed that thought is waves of vibration, starting from nerve centers, waves of smaller magnitude and greater frequency than those which constitute the X-ray."

"That I have read," the Doctor confirmed. "Certainly it sounds reasonable enough."

"It is the only way, theoretically, to explain the phenomena of thought transference—telepathy," said the Professor.

The Playwright banged the table with his fist.

"Why it's as clear as daylight once you think of it," he exclaimed. "Just as we send wireless vibrations from a sending to a receiving station, so we send thought vibrations from the nerve cells of one person's brain to another. It's perfectly clear."

"It is the only plausible theory, I think," said the Professor.

"You said you had proved it to be so," the Banker remarked. "I don't want to be skeptical," he added at the Professor's smile, "but everybody around this club is long on wild theories; I like to see something proved once in a while."

"Gentlemen," the Professor's look was very earnest, "if you wish I will give you proof of that theory. But first, I want to make clear to you that I am not psychic, not a medium, nor do I claim any power over the occult." There was a stir of anticipation among his hearers at these quiet words. "Spiritualism, so called, interests me, of course. But I am not a spiritualist; I don't want to be 'queer.' I am normal, I hope.

"But, gentlemen, with thought vibrations, with, let us say, intensive thinking, I have been able to do one or two rather remarkable things."

"Telepathy?" the Big Business Man suggested.

"No, not telepathy, though possibly akin to it. I'll show you." He stopped, then added slowly:

"Gentlemen, you may believe it or not, there is in the back of my mind an idea, an ambition if you will, that someday, entirely by the power of thought which I am developing, I shall be able, unaided by any other agency than my own brain, to create a living, breathing human being! By that, I—"

"Good Heavens," the Banker interrupted, "you mean with—"

The Professor seemed sorry he had spoken. He raised his hand deprecatingly.

"Gentlemen, I—that's only a vague notion I have been treasuring. If it interests you I—let me show you first the experiment I had in mind."

"There's a glass over there," he said, pointing to one of the smaller tables. "Will you hand it to me?"

The Very Young Man hastened to do so. It was a very tall, fragile tumbler such as lemonade is served in. At the Professor's direction, the Very Young Man set the glass in the center of the table, directly under the light. Around the table, all of them out of reach of the glass, the men sat staring at it intently.

"Watch closely," said the Professor. "I'm going to send thought vibrations against that glass."

The room became intensely quiet. The men sat leaning forward expectantly, seeming, most of them, to be holding their breath. The Professor fixed his gaze on the glass an instant, and then closing his eyes, sagged back limply in his chair.

"Just a moment," interrupted the Playwright suddenly. "You don't mind, do you? I thought we might raise the glass above the table—so that no other vibrations can possibly get at it."

The Professor smilingly agreed, and after conferring with the Playwright the Very Young Man left the room hastily. He was back in a moment with a ball of cord and a small silver tray with handles. This tray they hung by the string from the electrolier. It swung in the air some six inches above the table. On it they placed the glass.

When they had finished and taken their seats, the Professor relapsed into his former attitude, while the men around the table sat rigid, gazing fixedly at the shining, fragile glass standing on the tray in the full glare of light from above.

A minute passed and nothing happened. Another minute. The Banker shifted his feet noisily; his labored breathing was unpleasantly loud in the silence of the room. Then, with startling suddenness, there came a sharp crack and the tinkling sound of falling fragments of glass. There on the tray lay the tumbler, shattered into a score of pieces.

The Professor sat up again quietly, pressing his hands against his temples for an instant.

"It is very like a simple experiment in physics, really," he said quietly, as the men looked around at each other too amazed for words. "Those vibrations of thought, emanating from my brain, struck the glass and caused it to vibrate with them to such an extent that it was shattered. Such a phenomenon is not unusual. Only the fact that I used vibrations of thought instead of some others better known makes it remarkable."

"It's extraordinary," said the Big Business Man. "Perfectly extraordinary."

The Very Young Man cut down the tray and almost reverently gathered up the bits of broken glass.

"This spiritualism beats me," murmured the Banker, mopping his forehead. "It's too damned uncanny for me."

"I shouldn't call that spiritualism," said the Professor. "Spiritualism, or better let us say Psychical Research, as I understand it, deals with the intangible existence of our souls after death. In spiritualism, the trend of research is all from the tangible, the physical body, to the intangible, the astral body and the soul. My gropings of theory all lead the other way—from the intangible to the tangible."

"What do you mean by that?" asked the Banker in his most testily aggressive manner.

"The almost universal existence in matter of some form of vibration," the Professor answered, "and the marvelous things that have been accomplished with newly discovered vibrations, has made the subject one of great interest to me. I have studied its laws—well, as far as I could," he smiled, "and the principal conclusion I have reached is that no one knows very much about them.

"We know that sound-waves under normal atmospheric conditions travel ten hundred and fifty feet a second. Light, on the other hand, travels one hundred and eighty-six thousand miles a second."

"Some difference," murmured the Very Young Man.

"The X-Ray, the wireless, heat, other vibrations, all have their various properties; but all to a great extent obey recognized physical laws. Thought waves, however, so far as it has been determined, seem to transgress many of the physical laws that govern their vibrations."

"In what way?" asked the Doctor.

"Never mind what way," the Banker interrupted; "we'll take your word for it."

"Well, for instance, the impulse does not vary with the distance," smiled the Professor. "But I agree with you," he said to the Banker, "that is an unnecessarily technical discussion. And as a matter of fact, nobody knows much about it one way or the other."

"What's your theory?" asked the Banker.

"You make me rather hesitate to put it into scientific words," the Professor answered slowly, "since after all it is an extremely elusive idea—hardly so definite, even, that it could be called a theory. It is the belief, as I told you, that with the properly directed, intensive power of thought, a physical body can be created—matter having weight, length, breadth and thickness—matter occupying space. In other words, I am convinced that out of the intangibility of the things of which we are thinking, there can come, if we only knew how to produce it, a definite physical entity, solid, tangible; a living human being, for instance."

Silence greeted this calm statement, for the Professor's quiet voice, and his serious face and earnest manner, convinced his hearers that he was sincere.

"It's a romantic idea, certainly," the Playwright said, breaking the silence.

"How could it be done?" asked the Banker. "Assuming we knew how to think properly, what reason have you for saying it might be done. Is there any scientific basis for it?"

"I think there is," the Professor answered. "In the first place, gentlemen, let me make clear to you one point. My conception is that between things we call tangible and intangible there is no fundamental difference."

"Say that again," said the Banker.

"What I mean is simply this: I believe there are far more kinds of matter than the modern science of physics recognizes. Physics tells us that matter is anything occupying space; hence the necessity of occupying space, that is, being tangible, is, according to physics, an inherent property of matter. That I do not believe, in its strictest sense, to be so."

"Why not?" the Banker wanted to know.

"Physics tells us," the Professor went on imperturbably, "that no two bodies, that is, masses of matter, can occupy the same space at the same time. On the other hand, modern investigations in Psychical Research have led us to believe that the astral body—the wraith, 'ghost' you might call it, is composed of matter. It is very finely divided matter, it is impalpable, but it is matter, nevertheless. We all understand that a ghost can seemingly share the same space with a chair or a table. That is proved by the way in which wraiths have been observed to walk through solid objects."

"Then you mean to say that you believe that two bodies can occupy the same space at the same time?" the Doctor asked.

"I said 'seemingly,' " the Professor answered. "As a matter of fact, a ghost might walk right through this table," the

Very Young Man started involuntarily, "and it would not necessarily be breaking any law of physics. There is plenty of empty space between the molecules of this table; the more finely divided particles of the wraith would fit into those spaces, that is all."

"Like a glass of water filled to the brim," suggested the Playwright. "You can pour a spoonful of sugar into it without the water spilling over."

"Like that, exactly," the Professor agreed. "Let me give you another illustration more to the point. We all agree that this table is tangible, solid, matter occupying space. Let us now conceive another body, composed of matter, also. We'll call it X. It is right here now occupying some of the same space as the table. Understand me, gentlemen, I mean exactly that. This other body, this X, you are to conceive as being matter. It has weight, it has dimensions—how many we do not know, possibly four—it has shape, therefore, and it does occupy space.

"Now, gentlemen, assuming this X to be right here before us, there remain only our five senses, or possibly the proverbial sixth which we might term instinct, by which it can make known to us its presence. Now then, suppose you take our sense of sight. We can easily understand that if the vibrations of light that reflect from this object are below the infra-red or above the ultra-violet, we could not see them."

"I don't understand that," ventured the Very Young Man.

"It is known that there are rays vibrating too slowly for the human eye to see," the Professor explained. "They are called the infra-red. Others vibrate too rapidly, the ultra-violet. So you can conceive that if this was beyond either end of the scale we could not see it.

"Let us take the sense of hearing. Exactly the same holds true. There are sound vibrations both too slow and too rapid to be audible to human ears. With the sense of touch we can easily conceive this X to consist of particles of matter of such a quality as to be impalpable. It could be the same with the other senses.

"So, gentlemen, you must admit the possibility of there being another body here before us, the existence of which, with the physical senses God has given us, we have no perceiving means of becoming conscious."

"Why, then there might be a completely different other world right here around us!" exclaimed the Very Young Man.

"I see no reason to suppose that an impossibility," the Professor answered. "Perhaps, that is the fourth dimension. Another world—right here around us. There is only one way we can enter that world, gentlemen." The Professor paused a moment impressively. "Only one way we can enter that world—or bring anything from it into our world. That is by the power of thought—the power of the human intellect. That is the only way."

"What has all this to do with your original theory?" asked the Banker after a moment. "You said that thought waves could create a human being by their own action."

"Simply this," said the Professor. "I conceive bodies of this other world and of our own to be interchangeable. Both are composed of physical matter, only in a different state. The whole problem, as I see it, is one of vibration."

"What has vibration to do with the state of the matter?" asked the Big Business Man.

"A very great deal," the Professor answered. "Let me

explain. We have, let us say, three principal states of matter—solid, liquid and gaseous. Now there is a force, we call it molecular cohesion, that tends to hold the molecules of a mass together. In a solid substance, this force is very great; in a liquid, it is materially diminished; in a gas, it is changed to a repellant force; so that without the restraint of a container the molecules of a gas tend to scatter—the gas will disperse, in other words. Is that clear?"

His hearers nodded their comprehension.

"In addition to this attribute of molecular cohesion," the Professor went on, "we must conceive the molecules of every substance of our world to be in more or less rapid vibration. That is the phenomenon of heat. Now, between these two forces, molecular cohesion and this molecular vibration, there does exist some definite connection. This is proved by the fact that when we change the rate of molecular vibration, we alter the force of molecular cohesion and the body changes its state."

"I don't quite get that," said the Playwright.

"The most familiar example is ice," said the Professor. "Ice is a solid substance; its molecular cohesion is very strong; the vibration rate of its molecules is comparatively slow. We increase this vibration rate; the body changes its state. We have a liquid—water. We further increase the vibration rate and the substance changes its slate again. We have a gas. Understand me, gentlemen, these are not chemical changes—the substance chemically remains unaltered. It is purely a physical change—a change of state.

"Now, all this presupposes a change of temperature, and as you know, there are many substances that, instead of changing their physical state with a change of tempera-

ture, undergo a chemical change. The most common illustration of this is the phenomenon of combustion. But all
this applies only to matter as we know it in our world. I
have given the subject a great deal of consideration, gentlemen, and I have reached the conclusion that this relation
between molecular cohesion and molecular vibration is
far more fundamental than a question of temperature. I
believe, in other words, that, with substances of another
world, substances whose basic properties we have no means
of understanding, vibration properly applied can influence
molecular cohesion independently of temperature, and can
alter the physical state of the substance.

"Now then, gentlemen, let me go a step further. Vibrations, you can readily understand, are altered only by other
vibrations. That is one of the basic properties of vibration—
it is communicable."

"Like sound-waves make our eardrums vibrate," said
the Playwright.

"We can understand it best with sound, perhaps. But I
am sure it is clear to you all. Further vibrations are convert-
ible. Sound-waves make our eardrums vibrate; that is a
conversion of vibration. Thought waves made that glass
vibrate; the thought vibrations were first converted into
vibrations of the molecules of glass and then into vibrations of sound."

"How about when you broke the glass?" the Very Young
Man put in.

"When I broke the glass," the Professor answered, "I
took the first step toward changing its physical state. As I
understand it, by a sudden, very powerfully directed vibration, I partially destroyed its molecular cohesion; it was

shattered. Now, if I could have more skillfully directed this vibration, the glass would have completely altered its physical state. Its molecular vibration then would have been such as to render it invisible, invisible to us.

"It is exactly the reverse of this process, that I want you to imagine; a body in some inconceivable condition being so acted upon by thought vibrations that its state is altered until it becomes a recognizable substance belonging to our own world." The Professor paused to let this sink into the understanding of his hearers.

"And so I believe," he continued after a moment, "that whatever state of matter the bodies of this other world we have conceived may be in, that state may be converted to a state applying to our own world through the agency of vibrations. And, gentlemen, the only vibrations that can do it, and they must be properly directed, are the vibrations of thought!"

SITTING A LITTLE back from the table, to one side and slightly behind the Banker, was a young man who had taken no part in the discussion. He was under thirty, slim, muscular, blue-eyed, with wavy brown hair. His smooth-shaven face was bronzed as though by a tropic sun, and he had all the look of one who lives his life out of doors. He was the only one of the men not in evening dress. His name was Guy Bates; he was a two weeks' visitor at the club, a friend of the Doctor.

At the Professor's last words, he cleared his throat nervously, and hitching his chair forward a little, began in a voice that trembled with emotion.

"Gentlemen, I—I have been listening to your discussion for nearly an hour. It has been interesting, how interesting

Dr. Adams can understand a little. I have kept silent, and I want to thank you, Frank," he turned to the Doctor, "for respecting that silence."

There was a stir among the men at his quiet, earnest words.

"I have said nothing," he went on, "because—well, because this whole subject means so much to me. It is in a way sacred. Of such things, one cannot speak lightly to comparative strangers.

"I kept silent, too, because you," he addressed the Professor, "have been telling me things I always wanted to understand; and couldn't. Now you, you have suggested a possible solution to—to the greatest problem of my life. So in justice to your scientific theories and to—to myself, I must tell you what I know, what has happened to me." He stopped and looked around a little helplessly.

"I'm very glad you have decided to do that, Guy," said the Doctor quietly.

"I know you gentlemen will understand why I am willing to talk of such—such sacred things," said Guy Bates. "What I have to say will surprise you greatly." He hesitated an instant.

"Gentlemen," he began again, "I have been in that invisible world of which you have been speaking. And the girl I love is there now, waiting for me—and I—I can't get her out!"

2

"**WHEN I WAS** eighteen," began Guy Bates, after his hearers had recovered somewhat from their surprise at his first extraordinary statement, "that was eleven years ago, I left college and went to live with my uncle on his ranch in Texas. The thing really started there, I think. I suppose I was rather a dreamer, a romantic sort of boy, living mostly within myself. I was too introspective—my aunt used to tell me that; I was alone too much, and I spent too much time reading.

"I really don't quite know how it started. I remember I used to like to ride out on the range at night and sit for hours, alone, on my horse under the stars, thinking of the sort of girl I was going to find someday and marry. I suppose every boy does that more or less. I never cared much about girls, or at least I pretended I didn't, and I was always shy and diffident in their company. But I always had an ideal, and I used to like to get off alone with it, and dream.

"I remember the first time I really visualized how she should look, this girl I was going to marry. I was out on the range alone, at night, miles from anywhere; only the cattle around, and the stars overhead, and a little sliver of new moon. I remember being worried because I noticed it first over the wrong shoulder." He paused, smiling a little at the recollection.

"I got to thinking just how she should look. I knew I wanted her to be small, and slender, fragile almost. And with dark hair, big dark eyes, and a delicate, oval, wistful little face. And I thought she would have sometimes a scared, startled sort of look, as though life rather frightened her. I thought about her that way a long time, how long I don't know. Then I felt my lips moving and I heard myself say softly, 'I do want to find you someday, my little girl.'"

Guy Bates stopped again, his face flushed, and looked around at the solemn men listening intently to his words. All but one were considerably older than he—men of experience, who had accomplished things in the world—men who, many of them, had left youth and romance far behind them. But they were listening to him now, all of them, with sympathy and understanding, living their own pasts again, in the memories his words evoked.

"Gentlemen, I—I don't want you to think me silly, sentimental, talking like this."

"We don't, oh, we don't!" said the Very Young Man, in a voice hardly above a whisper.

"I'm not a boy anymore; I've grown up now. But I'm not ashamed of how I felt, how I looked at things then, or how I feel now. And I want to tell you the details, just as I remember them, because that is the only way I can make you understand what has been happening to me." He glanced at the Doctor appealingly.

"Tell it your own way, Guy," said the Doctor gently. "We understand."

"I had been thinking of her that way so long, and I guess

I had always visualized her the same more or less, that I knew just how she looked. It was very quiet out there alone in the hills, and yet somehow, when I heard myself speaking to her that way, I didn't seem to be alone exactly. I don't know quite how to explain how it was at first, but what I mean is—well, when I closed my eyes I could see her there before me. Yet when I opened them, she seemed to be there too—as though the vision persisted. When I spoke out loud that way, something answered me. It wasn't sound—I didn't hear it. But the words were just as clear and understandable as though I had heard them. It was a girl's voice, very soft and sweet and tender. I knew it was very soft and sweet; I knew just what its intonation was, just as your memory will give you the sound-memory of some familiar voice you haven't heard for weeks.

"And what she said was:

" 'You *have* found me now, because you have thought of me, created me.'

"All that summer she was hardly ever out of my thoughts for a minute. She got to be a part of my life, the only real part, it seemed to me then. I used to think of myself riding out over the prairie with her, or up North in the snow, or traveling in foreign lands. Sometimes at night, I dreamed of her; but mostly it was when I was awake, just thinking, daydreaming you call it, I guess.

"But the night of which I told you, when she spoke to me, was different. That wasn't just musing, just imagination. I felt somehow that she was really there, that night. Only I couldn't touch her, couldn't see her, could only think about her. Now, I know she was there—and you gentlemen know it, too. Only, she had no way of making her presence known except through my thoughts. I know now that she really did speak. Her voice did not make sound that my ears could hear. But it got to my brain and I knew about it, just as well as if my ears had heard it.

"That was how it started. The second time she came to me, I guess it was nearly a month afterward, it was late in the afternoon just before sundown I was sitting alone on the porch of the ranch house. They were driving in some steers down through the valley to the corral. I remember watching them. Then, remember thinking how pretty she would look—slim, girlish little figure on a spotted pony, riding around among the cattle and talking with the rough bunch we had down there on the range. And how they would adore her.

"Then, all at once, I knew she was beside me there on the porch. I think instinctively I put out my hand to touch her, but, of course, I couldn't. Then I heard her say—" He stopped and smiled.

"I suppose that's wrong, gentlemen. I didn't *hear* her. It's very hard to keep it straight, because you see it was just the same as if I had heard her. What she said was:

" 'I'm still waiting for you, dear. That's all there is for me to do—just wait and hope—for you. It's very, very lonesome—just waiting.'

"I couldn't answer that. I couldn't do anything, couldn't think of anything to say. I just sat and stared out over the valley to the hills where the big sun was setting all red and blurred and distorted.

"I was twenty-two, I think, before she came to me again. I was in Chicago then, where my uncle had sent me to work under my cousin in the office. That was the summer I first got started thinking about my invention. You tell them about that, will you, Frank?" he appealed to the Doctor.

"He's told me something about his invention," said the Doctor. "He has been working on it, thinking about it, for the past seven years. It's still nothing much more than a theory, is it, Guy?" The Doctor smiled at his young friend.

"I don't think it will profit us to discuss it now," the Doctor went on. "But I will say, if what he has conceived were ever accomplished, it would be one of the greatest, if not the greatest, discoveries of all time. But it has persistently eluded him, and there seems to be so delicate a thread to work upon that no one could help him—even if he were to ask for aid. He's not much nearer its solution now than he ever was. Is that all right, Guy?" The Doctor asked approbation of his explanation.

"Yes," said Guy. "I'm no nearer it now than I ever was." He smiled wistfully. "And she—she wants to help me with it." His voice trailed away and he sat staring out over the moonlit garden with set face and a far-away look in his eyes.

"Tell them, Guy," said the Doctor gently.

"The—the third time she came to me," resumed Guy, shaking himself together with a start, "was that first summer in Chicago. I woke up one morning just at dawn. My bed was near the open window. I sat up and looked out. The sun had not risen yet; the sky was all pink and rosy; the lake was placid like a great mirror, reflecting the colored clouds of the sky, and with a little mist hanging over it along the shore. You've seen it that way?

"I lay for a long time looking at the colors in the lake and thinking of her, and wondering just as I had always wondered every morning, whether I should meet her that day in the crowds of the city. Then she spoke to me, little tender words of greeting, and I knew she was sitting there beside me on the bed, sharing with me the beauty of the sunrise, the new day that was dawning for us both. I knew too she was all robed in white, with two great black braids of hair hanging down over her shoulders."

He was speaking so softly the men across the table hardly could hear him. The Banker gulped audibly and shifted in his chair uneasily, staring at his thin hands that lay locked in his lap.

"That was the first time I ever really talked with her. We talked there on the bed by the window, while the sun came up and the lake turned to blue and green, and the mist went away." He paused again. "Gentlemen, I—I just can't repeat to you what we said. You understand—I—....

"Then once, when we had been silent for a while, I—I threw out my arms to put them around her. She had been so real, sitting there, in my thoughts. And the things we had said, and all the wonderful promise of the coming day, this day we were sharing, I threw out my arms—and they came together in the empty air. Then I looked around the room and I hardly could believe it. I was alone. All alone, gentlemen, alone as I have always been—just—all—alone." His voice trembled and trailed away again; he put his hands to his face.

The Doctor rose and passing around the table sat on the arm of his young friend's chair with a hand on his shoulder.

"Just tell us the part that relates to our argument, Guy," he said. "What she told you about herself, and what you saw."

Guy looked up into the Doctor's kindly face and tried to smile.

"Just to be alone always, except for her and our thoughts—it's hard—sometimes, when you get to believing other—other things." He pressed his lips tightly together. "After that, she came to me often—nearly every day for a while that summer."

"You don't always speak to her out loud, Guy," the Doctor prompted.

"No, though I mostly do; it seems more natural that way, voicing things instead of thinking them. And it makes her answers seem more natural, too. I don't know why. But I don't always talk. Sometimes when she—she is with me, I just think what I am saying and she answers just the same. She doesn't know the difference, either. I found that out once."

"Tell them what she showed you," the Doctor suggested.

"It was about two years ago," Guy answered. His face grew wistful again, and the far-away look in his eyes came back. "She seemed much closer to me, always more tangible as the years passed. I used to think, back in the old days, that maybe she was a living girl here on this earth, and that someday, I should meet her face to face. Every morning when I woke up, I wondered if that would be the day.

"Then that time in Chicago while we were talking, I asked her who she was, what she was, and where I could find her. Then I knew—knew the hopelessness of it. For she answered:

" 'I'm nothing, yet, only the girl of your thoughts; your girl, waiting for you—just waiting for you to make me real.'

" 'Where are you?' I asked. And she answered:

" 'I'm here, right here, now; here with you. You cannot see me, cannot touch me. But you know I am here, you know that, don't you?'

" 'But you are not always here with me. Where are you then?'

"Gentlemen, she answered me in a voice of tenderness and longing that—that nearly broke my heart.

" 'When your every thought is not of me,' she said, 'then I have to go back home, back to the Realm of Unthought Things, and wait, just wait there, for you to bring me out again.'

"She gave a little sob. It was just a little while after that, I reached out my arms to touch her and found I was alone."

"Tell them what she showed you, Guy," said the Doctor again.

"When she told me, that way, about the Realm of Unthought Things, and I really came to realize it all, I just gave up hope for a while. You see, gentlemen, I had always believed she was a real girl, somewhere. And then when I—I knew—

"But she kept coming to me all that year, and the next, and the next. And she was always so sweet and gentle, and so tender—

"I told her all about my invention. She said once that she was going to try and help me with it.

"We went many places together, in our thoughts, because you see she could follow me that way easily. We romped and played together; forgot sometimes the terrible gulf that separated us in body. Then one day, it was just about two years ago, we discovered that I could follow her in her thoughts just as easily as she could follow me in mine; that she could take me places, too, by thinking of them, telling me about them.

"I was back on the ranch that summer. It was a hot night in August. I remember it as well as if it were yesterday—the night she first took me to the Realm of Unthought Things.

"I was out back of the ranch house, three or four miles, maybe. There's a little stream goes down through there; rippling over the stones, and there are falls in two or three places. I'd left my horse and was wandering along the edge of the brook. At the bottom of one of the falls, I sat down to rest. The water comes down a fifty-foot drop there into a big basin that's hollowed out broad and deep like a wash-bowl. There was a clump of trees behind me, and a rising ground on both sides of the stream that made it all dark and dim down there. There wasn't any moon that night, but the stars were very big and bright, so near-looking it seemed as though you ought to be able to reach up and pull them down.

"The water made a lot of noise splashing down from above, but everything else was quiet and solemn. I got to thinking how wonderful it would be if only she could be sitting there beside me, a living, breathing girl, touching me with her body, listening to the splash of the water and feeling the bigness of the world all round.

"And then she came. She said gently in that little wistful voice I knew so well:

" 'You brought me out again, dear, after so long a time. I'm glad, very glad.'

"We talked for a little while, and I made her know about the waterfall, and the purple hills, the wide plains behind, and the stars overhead. As she listened, I knew her eyes were very big and soft, and tender, always tender. Then finally she said:

" 'I think tonight, I can take you with me into my world. If you'll let me, if you really want to go.'

"Then she told me more about the Realm of Unthought Things, this other world, this world of hers. She made me see it clearly in my thoughts. As she talked, the sound of the water seemed gradually to fade. It got all dim and blurred. I could still hear it, but now it seemed coming from a great distance. The things around were faded, too—all vague and shadowy and confused; only what she was picturing for me, with her words, seemed real.

"Then she took me by the hand, pulling me to my feet. I can't say I felt her hand exactly, gentlemen, and yet, sometimes, sometimes, I really think I did—that night.

"We began to walk. I held her hand tightly, for the ground under my feet seemed unstable. We seemed to be floating along rather than walking. I think I was a little afraid at first, startled, but the feeling soon passed away.

"All the time, she kept talking, telling me what we were doing, where we were going, what I was to see. And all the time, the sound of the waterfall was murmuring in my ears, never growing less, just holding steady—a vague, quiet little hum.

"We floated along, for how many minutes or hours I have no idea, down through miles of dim, blurred valleys, past shadowy, shapeless rocks, and then out over wide, empty spaces that seemed to resound with our voices. But always, I was conscious of the splashing sound of water, and the purple hill in front always seemed to be there, although

I forgot it often, watching the other things drifting past, and listening to what she was telling me.

"Then, away up in front, there seemed to be outlines taking shape. We drifted onward and I saw there was a roof overhead, an immense spread of roof, how high above, I could not tell. I knew, too, there were walls about me although they were so far away I could not make them out. I seemed to be struggling now to make progress, not just floating, but moving against some resistance as though some force encompassed me, holding me back. It was a little as one feels walking shoulder deep in water.

"The girl's hand pulled me forward. 'The borderland,' she whispered. 'We'll be over it in a moment, then it will be easier. The borderland of the Realm of Unthought Things.'

"I struggled to keep my grip on her hand; it seemed always to be melting away between my fingers. I shoved my legs forward, squared my shoulders, breasting that invisible tide that threatened every instant to sweep me back.

"The girl talked very fast as we struggled; picturing vividly the things I was to see. Sometimes her voice faltered; then it would fade away, grow faint and elusive. Her fingers then seemed slipping, melting away, slipping out of my grasp.

" 'Think,' she cried once, sharply. 'Think, think hard. That great, unthought world up there ahead of us—think of it, hard, hard.' I caught a glimpse of her white face and her big, frightened eyes, shining in the gray of the light around. I remember, too, I could still hear the vague murmur of the waterfall beside me. Only I wouldn't listen, I wouldn't listen....

"Then all at once, the pressure relaxed. We swirled

forward, light as gossamer, and then settled down gently together in a little hollow of rock. She laughed triumphantly, a laugh that was almost a sob with the relief of it.

" 'We made it, dear,' she cried. 'I've got you here at last, here in my own world, where all the wonderful mysteries of the future lie waiting for you. I'm going to show them to you; everything, here in the Realm of Unthought Things.' "

3

THERE FOLLOWED A long silence, a silence that no one in the room seemed willing to break. The Banker cleared his throat nervously, exchanged a solemn glance with the Professor, and then gazed down again fixedly into his lap. Only the Playright moved; he rose silently to his feet after a moment and switched off the lights in the center electrolier. The room was plunged immediately into semi-darkness; the garden outside, with the moon almost overhead now, seemed to grow suddenly very bright and vivid by contrast.

"Her hand pulled me forward again," the low voice of Guy Bates resumed, "and we started together up the long incline that lay ahead. There was no resistance pulling at me now. I seemed to be wafted along like a bit of down floating in invisible currents of air, with no means of starting or stopping save by the tug or the restraining pressure of her guiding hand. I held it very tightly and it seemed now firm and real within my grasp.

"I looked around. The roof overhead, I could see plainly—a great, shaggy, gray expanse—stretching away into the dimness of the distance. It might have been a thousand feet above or a mile, or a thousand miles—I could not tell. The walls, too, of this vast cavern, for that is what it seemed to be, I thought I could make out vaguely. One of these walls, we were approaching as we drifted up the incline. But I noticed it never seemed to come nearer, never grew more definite as we went toward it, but always remained vague and blurred and shadowy—unattainable, unapproachable. Then I realized that it never could come closer, for I knew that the cavern was infinite in size, a universe of itself, illimitable in space.

"After a time, we left the ground and began to swerve upward, up and up, until we poised motionless, hanging in a great void and gazing down into the gray, illusive distance beneath like two aeronauts peering over the edge of their car down at the mist-covered earth they have left far below them. Then something stable, something palpable, seemed to come under us and we settled at rest upon it, close beside each other, her hand still tightly held in mine.

"In the gray half-light, the vast scene spread out below us was clearly visible. It seemed now, well, as if we were sitting upon some immeasurably high mountain crag, looking out to the far horizon over a limitless plain empty and gray as a desert waste; or as an unsailed sea might appear in the gray light of dawn viewed from a great height.

"Over our heads, the roof hung vague and distant as before. The great empty expanse beneath us, as I stared down into it, after a moment seemed empty no longer. Looking directly downward, very far below, I could make out now innumerable rows of gray, shadowy, motionless shapes extending in every direction; shapes, infinite in number, of every size and every contour. With the exception of that part directly beneath us, these shapes seemed piled one above the other in vast tiers, extending up to the roof, and to the sides and back into the obscurity of the unfathomable distance, like the countless galleries of some gigantic circular auditorium.

"How long I gazed, silent, at this awesome scene, I cannot say. I felt somehow omnipotent; like—like God might feel gazing down from above at the wonders of His own created universe.

"And then I heard her soft voice saying:

" 'All the wonders of the future, from now until the very end of time, lie waiting out there.

" 'All that the human mind will ever conceive from now through all eternity lies there, silent and fallow, waiting to be thought of.'

"Then she told me—told me that when my own world was created the Almighty created this other world too, this other state of matter that you gentlemen have been able to imagine by your scientific deductions. In it, He put every-thing that ever was to be thought of for all time."

Guy Bates looked around at his audience earnestly.

"Gentlemen," he continued, "at first, I couldn't quite seem to fathom the vastness of it—the—"

"Tell them what she showed you, Guy," said the Doctor.

"We sat there a very long time; at least, it seemed a long time and yet now I think, perhaps, it was only a moment. I remember that once while she was talking, she laid her hand upon my shoulder. I *felt* the weight of it resting there, I *felt* the grip of her fingers tighten suddenly as she realized that now at last I was like her, and to her impalpable no longer. She gave a little cry, a cry of happiness, and—and then I took her in my arms, holding her close, feeling her body firm at last within my embrace.

" 'I can show you this world now,' she said, when I had

released her. 'Because you are like me, just for now, but we must hurry.'

"The vague little fear that entered into her being must have come to me, also, for I became conscious that behind her was the outline of a silent purple hill and I remembered for an instant that there was always in my ears the faint murmuring sound of water splashing.

" 'Let us go,' she said hastily. We started together, floating gently downward. And then—then—....

" 'A very little thing, isn't it?' she said. I saw she was holding a tiny vial in her hand. We were standing upon the ground in a narrow aisle or passageway between two of the great tiers. The vial in her hand seemed very clear if I did not look at it directly, but when I tried to—to see it better, it seemed somehow to elude my sight.

" 'A very little thing,' she said again. 'But very, very wonderful. The Elixir of Life they will call it, perhaps ten thousand years from now. It is the conqueror of disease, and with it man will live a thousand years." She put the vial back in the shadow where it had been lying.

"Who will think of it?" I asked, but she shook her head, smiling sadly. 'They are trying now,' she said, 'but they have far, so very far to go.'

"We moved further along the passageway, past many blurred forms that were lying side by side in the lower tier.

" 'What is that?' I asked, stopping her.

"We were standing before a huge object that occupied an open space the height of several of the galleries. In form, as far as I could make it out among the shadows, it seemed to be—well, like one of our great ocean greyhounds, a very long, narrow body, towering high above our heads. At right angles to its length, and nearer one end, I could see a great spread of wing. It was as though some enormous dragonfly were lying on exhibit in a museum, as it might appear in the dimness of twilight.

"There seemed to be about this monster, lurking there so silent, a hidden sense of power, a latent energy, held lethargic and waiting only its time to awaken into life. There was about it, too, an almost pathetic air of helplessness as though it were bound down inert by invisible chains too strong to break.

"She led me around to where I could look straight up its great bulging side. I could see now many broad decks one above the other running its length, and between them scores of rectangular glass-covered windows, very large, some of them, opening into the hull. We stood nearly beneath one of the great spreading wings, and I could see above it, standing up from the center of the hull, a tall mast, with many sloping cables holding up the wing as a suspension bridge is held.

" 'That,' she said, 'is the greatest of all the Transatlantic Aeroplanes; the largest, the finest that ever will be built.'

"Then she pulled me away, telling me we must not spend so much thought upon one when there were thousands of other wonders I must see.

"We wandered on, back and forth through many passageways. Sometimes, we would float upward to the higher galleries. Always her hand, impatient of delay, pulled me forward, guided me, with only brief pauses when we stopped and for an instant, I gazed with a consciousness of knowledge that overwhelmed me, at the mysteries that no human mind had ever glimpsed. All the vast potentialities of human thought throughout the coming centuries were unlocked and laid bare before me.

"I followed the progress of medicine from the uncertain gropings of today, throughout the ages to the compounding of that marvelous elixir that was to make man almost immortal. I saw the advance of electricity, instruments that transported in a flash a semblance of the human body thousands of miles, as the voice is carried today; successive engines that were to do the work of the world, each one more efficient than all that had preceded.

"I followed the progress of astronomy. I stood beside the first telescope that ever was to make visible human life upon Mars. I stared, silent, at that gigantic microscope that first would open up the unknown realms of the atom and show the human life, infinitely small, existing there.

"I saw, too, that great projectile with which man was to accomplish his first successful trip into interplanetary space. I stood before it a long time, as long as she would permit."

Guy Bates paused an instant, then resumed.

"I think, gentlemen, of all I saw in the Realm of Unthought Things this bullet-shaped car was the most curiously impressive. Not of itself; it was not large, no larger than this room. But for what it stood, what it signified, the adventurous spirit of man leading him at last beyond the realms of his own world, out into space to conquer the mysteries of the universe.

"Nearby stood the huge gun with which the projectile was to be fired; and grouped around, I could see other smaller guns, the failures, yet showing now no hint of what was to be their fortune.

"Then as we traveled onward, back and forth through countless passageways, sometimes floating a myriad galleries upward or back again to the lowest, she pointed out scores of other still more wonderful things-to-be.

"She told me with eager, vivid words how the population of the earth was gradually to increase until every available bit of land was crowded denser far than India or China are today—hordes of swarming human bees in an outgrown hive. She pictured their problems of food, of clothing, of housing, of transportation, of the vast mechanical power needed to do their work, keep them alive, and the constant need of land that forced them at last to the verge of an exodus through space to undertake the invasion of another planet.

"As she talked, she pointed out the engines, machines, devices of every sort, all those multifarious appliances that the ingenuity of man was to devise for the solution of the pressing problems of his advancing civilization.

"She explained to me the methods by which the productivity of the soil was to be increased, the laws of nature for centuries considered unalterable, immutable, bent to man's will—a soil made immeasurably more bountiful to feed the added millions depending upon it.

"I examined in breathless wonderment the apparatus by which man was to look down into the solid earth as though it were a limpid pool with all its potential treasures lying bare to the sight, ready to be garnered.

"I followed the development of mechanical power; saw the age of steam supplanted by the age of electricity, always larger, greater, more intricate, more ingenious engines to do the world's work. Then I saw them all made insignificant,

useless, obsolete, by that great triumph of human reasoning and accomplishment when the power of the earth's
momentum was harnessed, as the power of a waterfall is
now harnessed.

"Then I came back toward the present, fifty thousand
years, and followed step by step the problem of fuel for this
increasing multitude. I saw the earth long since denuded of
its forests. I saw the coal deposits located and exhausted. I
saw the earth drained of its petroleum. I saw the discoveries
of other, better fuels, and then I saw them all succeeded at
last when, molecule by molecule, the water of the oceans
was disassociated into the gases of its atoms—the perfect
fuel in a storehouse inexhaustible.

"Then, too, when the still further need of land became
a gaunt, ghastly spectre stalking over the earth, I beheld
the omniscient genius of men altering the axis of the
earth, shifting it at will, until the polar ice melted, grass
and trees and flowers sprang up over the trackless wastes
made suddenly fertile in the heat of the newfound sunlight;
uninhabitable regions opening hospitable arms to the
pressing, restless crowd of humans that had been driven
to their edge.

"As I traveled onward through the centuries, I saw civilization reach its height, its very pinnacle of intricate development, its complex needs all ministered to by methods as
complicated as the problems they were created to solve. On
the summit I saw mankind, resting. Through the centuries
that followed, I saw it ceasing to strive, and, lying in the
protecting arms of nature, its every want supplied without
effort, it progressed no further.

"Slowly, insidiously, like the little rust that unnoticed

eats its way into the heart of steel, decadence began. Ambition lagged, no longer prodded by the sharp spur of necessity. Still, for centuries more, nature remained tolerant, fondling, caressing, weakening, by the very lavishness of her care, the idling mortals she was protecting.

"Further downward, on through the centuries, I saw civilization declining. Slowly at first, I sensed another change, vague, yet ominous as an approaching storm that gathers unseen below the horizon. Knowledge atrophied by achievement could no longer struggle with nature. The lash that drove man up the hill, was plied again, driving him down, down with ever hastening speed.

"Eons onward, I saw civilization in decay; and still further onward, mankind again in the primitive, a second childhood, shaking with a palsied old age and impotence. I saw its feeble, puerile mind again groping uncertainly with its simple problems, not conquering this time, not advancing, but always being pressed downward, yielding to the relentless hand of nature; fighting and losing a desperate, hopeless battle against extermination.

"At last I stood, shivering and cold, and saw a pitiful little rear-guard of humanity making its ineffectual stand, beaten down, and down, until at the very end, from the last, struggling, helpless mortal, nature remorselessly wrested the final life-spark.

"During all the time we had been passing up and down among the galleries, I frequently had noticed empty spaces on the tiers, between these sleeping mysteries of the future. I asked her about them.

" 'Over there,' she pointed at one of the empty niches, 'the Stevenson locomotive once lay. It waited all those centuries from the creation of the world, and then, at his call, it went to him.

" 'There, behind,' she pulled to one side a little, 'that little space held James Watt's first engine. And over there, see, on the tier above, there stood Fulton's steamboat—that folly at which they laughed and jeered.'

"Niche after niche she pointed out, naming all those familiar objects of my daily life, so familiar that they had become no longer wonders to me.

"We were floating down one of the lower passageways, when her hand pressing me back brought us to an abrupt halt and I heard her explanation.

" 'We have reached the present here, she said, 'that brief little birth-time for which they are all waiting.' She spoke hurriedly, softly, and her hand in mine trembled a little.

"Across the passageway from where we were hovering, there lay, half in shadow, what I could see was one of our large modern types of aeroplanes. As I watched, a portion of it seemed to detach itself from the rest, and struggled past us. I say struggled, gentlemen. At first glance, it seemed to be floating, just floating quietly along. Yet there was about its movement something that suggested conflict, as though its exit from this world were not easy, as though great effort were being exerted to draw it forth, to overcome something that was holding it back. It—it struggled past us, and disappeared down the passageway.

"And then as I watched, the aeroplane appeared gradually to dismember; it seemed almost to be melting away before my eyes. Then, in endless procession, from the tiniest bolt and screw to great portions of its body and planes, its parts fought their way past.

"After a time, she pulled me away, and we drifted onward. I noticed now where other shapes were lying, partly dismembered, where portions had gone and the mind of their creator had proven unequal to the task and abandoned them there, grotesquely deformed, shrouded monuments to the limitations of the human brain.

"We turned finally into a narrow passageway that I sensed was far off the beaten track, an inaccessible by-path in this realm of potential human achievement. I felt her hand again trembling in mine, and felt her pulling me forward hastily, almost feverishly. We turned several sharp corners, floated upward past a score of galleries, and came to rest in a dim little recess. She stooped and from out of the darkness at her feet lifted up a small cubical box. As she raised her head, I met her eyes; they were shining as I had never seen them shine before, and her face was transfigured with a look of triumph mingled with the love and tenderness that it always bore. I saw her whole body was trembling now, trembling with eagerness and with joy; and I felt myself trembling, too.

" 'You know what that is, dear?' she asked.

"I could find no words with which to reply, but I knew. She opened the box—and—and again I felt almost omnipotent as I stared down at the little mechanism within.

" 'Your invention,' she whispered vibrantly. 'Your contribution to the advancement of your world. There it is, all complete, except the parts you have thought of already, just waiting for you.'

"I put out my hand to take it, but she held it away from me.

" 'No,' she said, 'that is not possible—now. But someday you will have it. Some day you will bring it out, just by yourself, with the power of your own thought.'

"Then she explained every hidden detail of its working, until that unsolved mystery of my life, a mystery no longer, lay clear and lucid before me.

"At last, she closed the cover quietly, and with a wistful little sigh laid the box back in the obscurity of its shadowed nook."

Guy Bates let his voice die away; he was sitting upright in his chair, his hands hanging limply at his sides, his head thrown back, staring out into the garden with unseeing eyes.

"What was it she told you?" the Very Young Man ventured timidly, breaking the silence that followed.

Guy brought himself back with a start, looking slowly from one to the other of his listeners.

"Gentlemen, that is the—the curious part of all this. Have you ever recalled a dream and been positive that you had known certain things about it, had known them clearly in the dream, things that afterward eluded your reasoning mind? That is the way it was with me. I know now that she told me all this, I remember it vividly. I know that she made plain my own invention and scores of other mysteries of science.

"But now they are gone from my memory; only a consciousness of knowledge once possessed remains. I cannot even remember what they looked like. I see them now as vague, indistinct, blurred shapes, as I have described them so that you will see them, too."

A long pause followed. Finally the Doctor, with a parting pressure of his young friend's shoulder, rose to his feet, and crossed the room to the vacant chair in which he previously had been sitting.

"Go on, Guy," he prompted.

"We were drifting along one of the broad, lower passageways," Guy resumed, "just a little while afterward, I think. All at once, I felt myself faltering, lagging behind. My legs felt heavy and I—I seemed to be cold. It was my first remembrance of my body since we had crossed the borderland.

"She seemed to know my sensations as soon as I, for she stopped abruptly and faced me, the gathering moisture in her eyes making them great, luminous, shadowy pools.

" 'You must go back, now,' she said, as one who submits to a fate inexorable as death. 'You must go. I cannot keep you, now.'

"Then she put her hands upon my shoulders and again I enfolded her in my arms, little, delicate, fragile being, crushing her to me, as though by the very power of my embrace, I could hold her always. For a brief instant, everything was blotted out of my consciousness except the knowledge that I held her. Then the sound of splashing water faintly murmured in my ears. My arms around her seemed suddenly to grow heavy, solid. Her body seemed yielding with their pressure, melting, slipping away from them. She gave a faint little cry, and abruptly I released her.

"Then I felt myself being pulled forward, down toward the dim outline of a hill that lay ahead.

" 'Take me with you, please,' she implored. 'Take me back with you, just a little way over the border.'

"I seized her by the hand, trying and failing to keep it firm within my grasp.

"Back to the borderland I was swept, unresisting, yet struggling, too, against a power, a *something*, that strove to hold me back. My hand pulled her forward and I talked to her steadily, with swift, incoherent words. But all the time my mind was drifting, pulling away from the sense of my words. The knowledge of a silent purple hill, and always that ever-increasing sound of splashing water, intruded into my thoughts.

"We entered the borderland and again there began that fearful struggle—a contest this time in which I took no part. It was as though I were a bit of cork, tossed and buffeted on a stormy sea, the desired prize of an opposing wind and tide.

"For some indefinite time, the strife continued. Then I was swept over the borderland out of the tempest into a calm and peace and silence only broken by the sound of water falling, a sound that soothed and lulled my tired senses.

"I still held her eluding hand.

" 'I'm here,' she said once, 'still here with you, dear.'

"Suddenly I remembered I was cold, and the muscles of my back hurt. Before I could prevent it, her hand slipped completely from mine. I heard her give a little moan, a low, yearning, hopeless cry of resignation.

"I turned around to her with an effort, conscious of a pain in one of my elbows. The sound of the water splashing seemed all at once to grow very loud, roaring through my head.

"She was gone. A sudden sense of loneliness made me shiver. One of my legs was stiff. I lifted it up off the other, and tried to bend it a little.

"Both my elbows were sore from where they had been holding my weight upon the ground. I sat up. Before me lay the silent outline of the hill, with the first faint pink glow of dawn tinging the sky behind it. I could just make out a little clump of trees at its foot. Beside me, the little stream flowed past; overhead, the myriad stars were paling in the growing light. It was all very silent and solemn, silent save for the waterfall splashing down into its shallow basin and droning noisily in my ears.

"A chill feeling of moisture was in the air—the mist of morning. I rose to my feet, stretching, for I was stiff and sore all over, and cold.

"Half an hour later I was back at the ranch house."

4

GUY BATES CEASED speaking. For a moment, there was complete silence in the room. Then the Doctor rose quietly and again switched on the center electrolier, flooding the table with light. The men around the table, sitting most of them limply in their chairs, shivered a little, shifted uneasily, or sat up stiffly, blinking in the sudden glare. They had been living for one brief hour in another world, a world of romance that men of their type seldom enter.

The matter-of-fact way in which the narrative ended, and this abrupt lighting of the room, brought them to themselves with a start. They knew, now, this was no fantasy they had heard; to their trained analytical minds its scientific meaning was clear. With the possible exception of the Very Young Man, they were more thrilled, sitting now again in their own world of realities, with its scientific aspect than with its romance.

The Doctor sat down again in his chair.

"I'm very glad you have told them, Guy," he said quietly.

"Is that all?" asked the Big Business Man.

"That's all," Guy answered. "She never took me there again, although she still comes out to me, sometimes."

"That's the most remarkable story I ever heard," the Playwright declared emphatically. "Perfectly remarkable." He fumbled in his pocket for his cigarette case and when he produced it the Very Young Man immediately borrowed a cigarette.

"It *is* a remarkable story," said the Professor thoughtfully, "and I think, gentlemen, it fits in very well with the theories we were discussing."

"It proves everything," said the Playwright, "everything you said, to my way of thinking. But it doesn't help us with the problem you proposed; it doesn't help us get that girl out of that invisible world, make her concrete, make her a living, breathing human girl here on this earth."

The Big Business Man looked at Guy Bates sympathetically and sighed, murmuring something under his breath.

The Professor smiled gently.

"I don't think our young friend here needs condolence nor protestations from us in order to understand how deeply we all feel for him. His situation—"

"Oh, can't we get her out, can't you suggest how we might get her out?" The Very Young Man's face behind a cloud of cigarette smoke was flushed and eager.

"I don't know," the Professor answered slowly. "I believe it possible. I myself have accomplished so many things with thought vibrations, and yet—the limitations to what I have done, the blank stone barrier I have reached so often—"

"I told you the story," said Guy, the wistful note crept into his voice again, "I told you because, with the power you have developed I hoped you might help me."

"If I can, of course," the Professor answered. He drew his chair closer to the table and leaned forward with his elbows upon it.

"Gentlemen," he began earnestly, "perhaps there is something we can do. I do not know. But I think first we should examine these experiences of our young friend from every possible angle, analyze them carefully. Perhaps, with his help, for in the case of this girl, at any rate, he seems possessed of a power certainly stronger than mine, perhaps we may be able to accomplish something."

The Banker, apparently, had been in a brown study, staring into his lap and taking no part in the discussion. Suddenly, he raised his head.

"If we are going to analyze the story," he said, addressing the Professor, "there is a discrepancy I should like to point out."

"That's what we want," said the Professor.

"As I understand it," the Banker went on, "he found this Realm of Unthought Things to be located in some sort of immense cavern. He said, if I remember rightly, he could see its roof, and its walls dimly in the distance. Then he said it was a cavern infinite in size, limitless, like our own universe, or like space itself. That's the impression I got, anyway.

"It occurred to me at the time, only I didn't want to interrupt, how could he see these walls if this realm was limitless, infinite in size?" The Banker relapsed in his chair. It was an unnaturally long speech for him; he spoke earnestly, and yet in his characteristic way, triumphantly, as he propounded this question.

The Professor smiled.

"I can understand how that would sound to you, George," he said. "Perhaps not even he could explain it, for he has told us his memory of what occurred, exactly as he remembers it—not what his mind has reasoned out. But your question is certainly pertinent and I think I can make the point clear. The difficulty is you are trying to conceive of a scene being viewed with human eyes, subject to the limitations of human sight. He says he saw this cavern, saw this roof, these walls. So instinctively, we all conceive the scene as we would view it with our sense of sight. That is natural. But, gentlemen, I believe you can realize it is a wholly false conception.

"What Mr. Bates saw, we must use that word as our language contains no other more suitable, what he saw was not seen with his eyes. They were fixed upon that hill across the river which he mentioned several times. He saw with his thoughts, the mental pictures he received had nothing to do with his sense of sight, just as what he heard the girl say was not heard with his ears, which heard only the waterfall."

"That's simple enough," said the Playwright.

"Now then, gentlemen," the Professor continued, "let us be careful to keep that one fact firmly before us, otherwise we shall go far astray in our reasoning.

"You can appreciate then, that if we imagine *seeing* without the limitations of our sense of sight, this narrative becomes far more understandable. Seeing with thought, that is the mental pictures that thought can give us, is not unique; we all do it all the time. Most certainly, the limitations of space are absent.

"Let us give you an example. You dined, let us say, last year in two restaurants, one here in this club, directly beneath our feet, one in Calcutta, nearly halfway around the world. You can recall those two dinners vividly. You sit here, silent, and you gaze out there at that garden. You think of the dinner you had downstairs. You remember the friends who were with you, how they looked, what you ate. The scene comes to your mind. You see it clearly. Not with your eyes, gentlemen. They only see that garden out there.

"Then your thoughts go to Calcutta. You can see the scene there in that restaurant in Calcutta just as clearly, just as vividly, as you can the one right downstairs.

"So, gentlemen, you can understand the limitations of space are absent in thought and you can conceive how, with his mind receiving the thought vibrations, the stimuli of this girl's mind, he could see the walls of this limitless cavern."

"Thought has no time either, has it?" asked the Big Business Man.

"I don't know," replied the Professor. "No one knows the speed with which thought vibrations travel. But it is certain that even light, with its almost inconceivable speed, is a pitiful laggard beside thought."

"That's easy to understand," cried the Playwright. "Think of one of the remote stars and your thought is there as you speak. Yet they tell us it takes light thousands of years to travel that distance. Or you can think of Noah entering the Ark many centuries ago just as quickly as you can think of the trolley car you boarded this morning."

The Professor smiled with amused tolerance at the Playwright's sophistry, but said nothing.

"There was another thing," continued the Banker. "Bates said things seemed blurred. Why was that? When I picture anything mentally its outlines are clear, not blurred."

He did not speak triumphantly this time, but simply, as one who seeks information on an interesting subject.

"I should explain that," the Professor said, "as due to the

fact that his mental pictures were not received directly from his own thoughts, but through the medium of hers. In this transference of thought, we can appreciate that inevitably something must have been lost. In all the experiments that have been made so far between two people of this earth, exactly that has happened. Thought images transferred from one brain to another have even been inverted; a picture of an arrow sent with its head pointing one way has been received with its head pointing the other. You've read of that, haven't you?"

"Yes, I have," said the Doctor, to whom the Professor appealed.

"Sometimes images are distorted by thought transference," the Professor added.

"These weren't," said Guy. "They were just a little blurred, not distorted."

"Like a piece of glass with a thin film of grease spread evenly over it," suggested the Playwright. "That blurs an image a little, but it doesn't distort it."

The Banker seemed to have still another question troubling him.

"Say it, George," the Doctor prompted with a smile.

"I was just thinking," the Banker began after a moment's hesitation, "our young friend here seems pretty well educated certainly, and intelligent," he glanced at Guy quizzically, "but to hear him talk ordinarily, you'd never suspect him of being an orator, would you now?"

"I hadn't thought of that," said the Doctor quickly. "You certainly were eloquent, Guy, with that story as you told it tonight."

"That's what I mean," added the Banker. "It didn't sound normal to me."

"That's just the point; it wasn't normal," put in the Professor quickly. "It was quite abnormal. You can readily understand, gentlemen, that the experiences he was describing were a thought-journey so vast, so stupendous, that in his emotion in telling it, picturing it for us, his subconscious mind, with all its latent ability for eloquence, spoke for him."

"He was inspired, in a way, you mean," interpolated the Big Business Man.

"I believe he was," the Professor nodded emphatically. "Exactly that."

Obviously, Guy had been entirely unaware of the display of such a power, for he seemed confused by the turn the conversation had taken, and only shook his head with a smile.

FOR NEARLY HALF an hour longer, the discussion continued, each of the men arguing the case from his own point of view, giving his ideas, his theories, and promptly being assailed by some other member of the little gathering. During all this time, the Professor said little, sometimes sitting apparently in deep thought, sometimes smiling in amusement as he allowed some totally false premise to pass unchallenged.

Then quietly he spoke.

"Gentlemen," he began, "I think there is something we can do to throw light upon this matter, something that may bring us more definite results than mere theoretical discussion."

The room became quiet at once and the Professor went on:

"I believe, it is my opinion," he seemed to be choosing his words carefully, "that not only theoretically but practically, the transmutation of this thought-girl into a woman of human clay is possible for us to accomplish."

Seeing the expression on Guy's face, he hastened to add:

"I don't want to hold out any false hopes; we may not succeed. But, nevertheless, I do believe it is possible.

"I think, gentlemen, the line of reasoning we should follow is this: Let us assume first that everyone has, or can develop to a greater or lesser degree, some power with his thought vibrations. You have seen a little of the unusual physical effect of thought vibrations in my case. That power, if you care to call it that, I believe to be the result of only two qualities of mind. First a brain trained to think constructively, to concentrate, to be more completely under the control of the will than is usual with the average person. Let us call it intensive thought. That describes it as well, perhaps, as any other term. Secondly, practice."

"What good does practice do if you don't know what methods you are to use?" asked the Big Business Man.

"There you have me, Will," the Professor said, laughing. "I must confess, I do not know. Perhaps, I am wrong on that point. But I think not. I believe this power properly to direct thought vibrations does not come of an abnormality of mind. I believe it is acquired through practice, instinctively found, hit upon by accident, let us say. I believe that is how I acquired it at any rate.

"Now, let us take the case of Mr. Bates here. That he has a power analogous to mine no one can deny. It differs, however, in this respect. While mine, to a limited extent, is operative upon objects of our own material universe, his has, in the case of this girl at any rate, been able to cross over into the other world.

"We can easily understand, gentlemen, how that came to pass. His mind, through constant thinking of her day after day in his youth, subconsciously, probably, all through his boyhood, became, in its thought vibrations, so attuned to hers, *en rapport*, we might say, that communication was established.

"Throughout the years that followed, this continuous concentration of thought has given him a greater and greater power over her. He has been unknowingly struggling to draw her out of the state of matter in which she now exists. But the power of his thought has been unequal to the task. Perhaps, it always will be; perhaps, the power of any single intellect is inadequate to perform such a seeming miracle."

"What are you getting at?" asked the Banker abruptly.

"What I am getting at is this. I propose, gentlemen, now, with your approval, to try the experiment of using the simultaneously exerted forces of two brains, his and mine. More than that, the power of yours, and yours," he pointed a decisive finger at each of the men in turn.

"In effect, gentlemen, I propose to determine the result of a combined effort of intensive thought upon the part of us all, a united effort of our wills, our intellects, our thought vibrations, directed simultaneously at this girl in an endeavor to break the chains that are binding her to the invisible world."

"Good God!" ejaculated the Banker under his breath.

"Can we do it, do you think?" the Big Business Man asked.

"I have no idea what the result will be," the Professor answered in his same quiet, even tone. "But there seem to be no reasons why we may not anticipate some slight result at least—some new phenomenon that may give us a further basis to work upon. If you gentlemen wish, shall we try it?"

"You must tell us what to do," said the Big Business Man, as the others nodded acquiescence.

"Shall I turn off the lights?" The Playwright, with an eye to the best dramatic effect, was looking around the room uncertainly.

"Well, yes, I suppose so," the Professor answered. "We may be able to concentrate better that way."

The Very Young Man switched off the lights in the elec-trolier, plunging the room again into semi-darkness. The men settled back in their chairs, all but Guy Bates, who with flushed face sat bolt upright, trembling violently.

"Now then," said the Playwright, "we must get this right. What do we do first?"

"Gentlemen," began the quiet voice of the Professor, "you are to visualize the face and form of this young girl, as Mr. Bates describes her to us. Seat yourselves as comfortably as possible, close your eyes, allow nothing of your physical surroundings to intrude upon your thoughts. You, Mr. Bates, will picture this girl as vividly as you can. Speak softly, as evenly as possible, without emotion or sudden change of intonation.

"You, gentlemen, must all endeavor to think of nothing except the mental picture that these words create. Pay no heed to the passing of time. Entertain no thoughts of speculation as to what may happen. Think of nothing except this girl as his words picture her for you. Get her image clearly before you. Dwell upon it. Concentrate upon drawing it visually closer. Make yourselves feel it is here, that you are seeing it with your eyes, its every detail distinct and definite. Do I make myself clear?"

Again they signified assent.

"You, Mr. Bates," the Professor went on, "will be careful, so far as you can, that each of us receives the same mental picture. Leave no doubt in your words as to just exactly what she looks like. Say the same thing over and over, if you think it necessary. Linger over every detail; make your description as complete, as vivid, as you possibly can. As you talk, conceive her yourself, here in this room before you. Try and draw her here. Try consciously, as no doubt you often have, to bring her to you. Do you understand?"

"Yes, sir, I do understand," Guy answered tremulously. "I'll try."

"Tell us about her as she looked that morning in Chicago," said the Very Young Man in a voice hardly above a whisper.

The men relaxed in their chairs with eyes closed. Only Guy Bates sat upright, rigid as a statue, staring straight before him.

THERE WAS SOMETHING of weirdness about the scene in this darkened room. The silver garden outside shimmered in the moon rays. A few black-coated men and girls, in filmy dresses of white, wandered about its paths, or sat whispering in the shadows of its arbors. Sometimes a subdued ripple of laughter would float out into the night air, laughter that beat unavailing against the wall of science with which the darkened enclosures so near them was surrounded.

After a moment Guy began speaking, in a low monotone, almost as one who speaks in a trance. His voice, low as it was pitched, carried to the furthest corners of the hushed room. Minute after minute, he droned his monotonous hypnotizing words. One of the men drew a long audible sighing breath, another shifted his feet, and from another came a stifled cough. Then as the image of this little dark-eyed girl came more and more vividly to the mind of each of the men, they sat silent, some rigid, tense, hands tightly gripping their chair-arms; others partly relaxed, all seeming scarcely to breathe. Yet the brain of each was a whirling dynamo, sending out its power, restless, active, striving with its all-pervading force to seek out this girl of their thoughts from the unknown that held her enchained.

The atmosphere of the darkened room seemed pervaded now with an elusive, soundless, motionless activity—a vague portent of struggle, as the air of a soft summer night is often charged with the coming electrical storm.

Like a statue with moving lips, staring with wide, unseeing eyes, Guy addressed his silent audience. The shadows of the room, the moonlighted garden through which he stared, held nothing for his vision save the image of a gray rectangle of casement, the outlines of a bed, and a slender white-robed girl sitting upon it.

He found himself waiting, in his pauses, for the sound of her voice. Then, detached, as one who sits apart and follows a speaker's words, he heard his own voice taking up again, in endless repetition, those futile phrases so wholly inadequate to paint the glory of her beauty.

OUT THROUGH THE little, shadowy windows, over the silent coloring lake of his thoughts, he could see the stars, hanging in their field of blue. A sudden noise beside him obtruded itself. He blinked and became conscious of the gleaming garden, with the same brilliant stars in the blue above it. His voice faltered and died away. He turned his head; in the dim light he could see the form of the Banker at his elbow. Then his gaze shifted again to the moonlit night outside.

Just beyond the threshold of the room, in the silver radiance outside, he saw a faint nebulous figure undulating slowly toward him. It crossed the threshold and then, as it came forward with a slow, measured, hasteless step that had about it nothing of mortal movement, he saw it shining in the nearer darkness with the glow of its own light—the slender figure of a girl, with two long braids hanging forward over her shoulders, jet-black against the white of her flowing robe.

He put his hand upon the Banker's arm suddenly and started to his feet.

"Look," he cried tensely, "over there! Can't you see her over there?" He pointed a trembling hand toward the entrance of the garden. His face was ghastly white; his eyes gleamed with a strange light.

The silence of the room was broken by the sound of shuffling feet as the men looked up and followed the direction of his hand. Some of them sat transfixed at what they saw; others jumped to their feet with muttered, incredulous exclamations, gazing in amazement at the figure that was advancing slowly into the room, and momentarily becoming more tangible.

When she had nearly reached the table, the girl paused, and standing with it between her and Guy, appealingly stretched out her arms toward him. Every detail of her face was clearly defined to them all. Except for the light about her, a dim, silver radiance, she might have been a human girl standing there before them. Her frail figure, in its flowing robe, was slender with the slenderness of a girl-woman, hardly more than a child. Her head was small; her black hair, parted in the middle, fell in two long braids nearly to her knees. Her face was small and oval; her eyes unnaturally big, held a frightened, timid look, like the soft eyes of a startled fawn. As she gazed across the table at the tense face of Guy, he could see they were glistening with tears, and that they held a look of yearning, of patient, plaintive appeal, ineffably tender, sweet and womanly. Like Niobe, she stood: a silent, drooping, pathetic little figure, with quivering lips and tears welling up in her eyes.

The Doctor found his voice.

"Speak to her, Guy, speak to her," he said, in a sibilant whisper.

The girl's lips were moving now. Two little soundless syllables they seemed to frame, the word "Good-bye." The look in her eyes grew more imploring. Then her body seemed to swirl sidewise, and, as though she were being drawn back against her will, she began moving away, keeping her arms outstretched and always facing Guy.

A definable, progressing change in her now became apparent, a lessening opacity, an increasing mistiness seeming to cloud the clearness of her aspect.

As she passed across the room, a sharp exclamation of

shock burst from the Banker, for her form passed directly through a chair that had barred its progress.

Then, while every man in the room faced her, she floated gently upward, with outstretched arms held down, as some wingless angel might hover in a dream of fairyland. As she poised in the air above them, her form seemed to blur, to diffuse, to evaporate into nothingness, wrapped in its own expiring glow. For a single instant, the plaintive, wistful little face, with its big, imploring eyes and black crown of hair, remained visible, and then was gone.

FOR A FULL minute after the disappearance of this briefly visible entity the power of their thought had produced, the men stood without power of speech or action. Then, abruptly, the tension snapped. They dropped into their chairs again, exchanging hurried comments, speaking softly, for the room still seemed pregnant with the invisible, the mysteries of the unknown they had been assailing.

The Banker shakingly switched on the light, not only the center electrolier, but those at the sides as well. The men seemed to bask in the glare with a grateful return of normality, welcoming it as the horror-frozen wayfarer in a haunted house welcomes the warmth of the rising sun.

"Sixty years," said the Banker, mopping his forehead, "and never before have I seen a ghost."

"That was not a ghost." The Professor spoke with an excitement unnatural to him. "Gentlemen, don't you understand that was not a ghost, no manifestation from the spiritual world?"

"It went right through that chair; I saw it." The Playwright looked around for confirmation of this statement.

The Big Business Man leaned toward the Banker and

began an excited aside. Guy Bates, of them all remained as he had been, staring straight before him, the memory of his thought-girl still persisting. The Very Young Man put out a hand and laid it timidly on his arm, withdrawing it hastily as Guy turned to him and tried to smile.

"Gentlemen," the Professor continued, striving to hold his voice quiet, "we have succeeded to a degree far greater than I anticipated. That—ghost—as you call it, was not a ghost; it had nothing whatever to do with such phenomena. It was not the materialization of a spirit, but the physical body of a living girl, made visible to our sight by the power of our thoughts. That we could not entirely break the chain, could not hold her, could not bring her completely into our own state of being, is not a fault of method, but of degree. We shall succeed, gentlemen. I am willing to tell you that now, for I believe it thoroughly. We shall succeed."

"Oh, I hope so; I do hope so," the Very Young man murmured; his eyes never left Guy's face.

"How did that apparition differ in looks from a ghost? I don't mean to dispute your statement," the Banker added earnestly; "I'm just asking for information."

"It looked absolutely different," the Doctor put in quickly.

"How do you know?" cried the Playwright. "None of us ever saw a ghost, did we? How do we know how one looks?"

"We've read the descriptions of people who say they have seen them, haven't we?" asked the Big Business Man warmly. "They all agree, in general. If we don't know what a ghost looks like we ought to."

"A spirit apparition is transparent," the Doctor declared. "You all know that this one wasn't; it was opaque."

"I noticed that," confirmed the Big Business Man. "I saw her pass that picture, and the picture was blotted out."

"That's the point exactly," the Professor agreed. "As I understand it, gentlemen, what happened is this: we looked up at Mr. Bates's exclamation. I first saw the girl as she came through that doorway apparently entering from the garden. I assume you all did, too." They nodded.

"Her appearance then was something like that of a wraith as it is usually described. It had about it a certain mistiness; it seemed nebulous, in other words. But as she advanced, if you will remember, her figure rapidly lost this nebulous look. It took on an appearance of tangibility, of solidity. That was about the time you noticed her pass in front of that picture, blotting it out." He turned to the Big Business Man.

I noticed that too," said the Playwright, "when she passed in front of you. I was standing over there."

"When she reached the table here and paused," the Professor went on, "her aspect, except for the radiance surrounding her, was, to me, almost that of a normal living girl. Gentlemen, I believe that for one brief instant then, if we had touched her we should have found her palpable; if we had lifted her up, we would have felt her ponderable in our arms."

"But she went right through that chair. I saw her," protested the Playwright.

"She did not," the Professor contradicted. "Not then, if you'll remember. That was afterward."

The Playwright agreed he was mistaken.

"As she stood here," the Professor went on, "and whatever power it was we were exerting over her began to wane, her state began rapidly to change. She was opaque at one time, I could see that clearly. Then she became translucent, then transparent. It was when she began moving away from the table, and her body already had partially returned to its former condition, that she passed through the chair. Previous to that time, she had seemed to avoid the articles of furniture. Such an avoidance has become so usual a thing in our own lives, it is natural you may not have remarked it. Do you believe I am right, gentlemen?"

There was no voice of dissent raised now to his reasoning.

"Why couldn't we keep her here, do you suppose?" the Very Young Man asked.

"I do not believe," the Professor answered, "that even for that brief instant I have mentioned, here at the table, we succeeded in changing her absolutely to a state of being similar to our own."

"I saw her lips move but we couldn't hear the sound of her voice," the Doctor put in.

"Exactly. I conceive her to have been at that moment in some state midway between our own and the one to which she now has returned.

"She was then hovering between the two, the forces pulling against her were balanced. Then ours lessened, she was drawn away, back into the world of the invisible."

"How are we ever going to hold her then," the Big Business Man asked, "if that is so? We may bring her here to our world, and then, if ever we relax our thinking of her she will slip back again."

"I do not understand it that way," the Professor answered.

"Do you know anything of the laws of inertia?" The Big Business Man nodded doubtfully.

"It is my opinion," the Professor went on, "that the laws with which we are contending in this transmutation, are similar to the laws of inertia. Those laws say that a body in motion will remain in motion unless acted upon by a restraining force; and that a body in a state of rest will remain at rest until some force is applied."

"I don't see the analogy," said the Playwright.

"Simply this. I conceive that the initial thought-power necessary to bring a body even partially out of this other world to be extremely great. The impetus thus given could not, you can appreciate, carry it forward through whatever successive changes of state are required, because the restraining force of its own world is never relaxed.

"But, once it completely enters our own physical state, I believe that other-world force will be powerless."

"Why?" asked the Banker.

"Because then the body will have acquired an inherent force of its own—the force with which all matter is endowed here, the force that holds it in its own state. That, gentlemen, is a force well known to physics. Do I make myself clear?"

"You believe then," said the Big Business Man, "that if we can once endow this girl's body with physical qualities similar to our own, so that the same physical laws apply to it that apply to us, it will have no more tendency to revert to this other world than we ourselves have?"

"I do mean that, just exactly that."

"How are we going to do it?" the Banker wanted to know. "We've tried our best and failed."

The Professor hesitated a moment with wrinkled brow, seeming a little at a loss just how best to convey to them his convictions.

"Gentlemen," he began finally, "our experiment just now was predicated on the belief that there must be some peculiar advantage in using, simultaneously, the thought-waves of several brains." He took off his eyeglasses, holding them in his hand and gesturing with them occasionally. "The results we have obtained seem to justify that assumption."

"So far as Bates was concerned we accomplished nothing new, did we?" the Playwright asked. "He has seen the girl many times before; he told us so."

Guy shook off his preoccupied air with an effort at this mention of his name.

"I never saw her like that before," he said simply.

"That's just the point," the Professor added quickly. "He never saw her like that before, gentlemen, because this time he saw her with his eyes, his sense of sight, not with the eye of his mind. She was here, gentlemen, not in our thoughts, but actually here, in this room, visible to us all. That is a tremendous advance; it puts an entirely new aspect on the matter."

"If we could only change her completely to our state—" The Big Business Man seemed talking to himself, ending with a long sigh.

"As I conceive the problem now, gentlemen," the Professor went on, "there seems to be no new element in it since we made this experiment. We failed, yes. But nothing that occurred would seem to indicate that our reasoning was wrong. We were successful, perfectly, as far as we went, but we did not go far enough."

"You mean we did not think with enough concentration—we need more practice?" asked the Playwright.

"Possibly that. Yet, gentlemen—well, it seems logical, even obvious, to me, that since we have been able to make so great an advance, and in exactly the right direction, by using several intellects instead of one, that the ultimate, final achievement of this transmutation may be attained by using still more mentalities than we have here, mentalities whose combined power far exceeds ours."

He stopped. There was a brief moment of silence.

"Why, naturally, that's the way to do it," The Big Business Man said, as though the idea had always been in his mind.

"How can we do it best?" the Doctor asked—for after a moment's argument every man in the room seemed to accept the Professor's reasoning as correct and was eager to try it out.

"Suppose we write a form letter to a thousand people," suggested the Big Business Man, "asking them all to read an enclosed description of the girl at a specified moment, and then have them all simultaneously trying to visualize her?"

"Why not have it published in some special edition of the newspapers?" the Playwright amended. "Then we could appeal to the whole city to think of her at once."

The Playwright's suggestion met with enthusiasm from several of the company. The Professor listened to their excited comments and then interrupted quietly.

"Your plan gentlemen is ingenious, and of course no one can say but that it would be successful. It is my opinion, however, that what is needed is not so much a vast number of minds, as a comparatively few, selected because of their strength of intellect, their ability to concentrate effectively."

"You're right," the Doctor emphatically agreed.

"It seems to me that by using so many minds, such diversified mentalities, we would be apt to scatter our forces, weaken our attack, perhaps, by the very multiplicity of the thought waves we sent out. Then, too, we could have no assurance of what kind of thoughts would be created. In some individual minds, undoubtedly, our printed words would create images of the kind that could not aid us. More than that, if in sufficient number, they might be positively harmful. You understand what I mean, I'm sure."

Guy shuddered at the implication of the Professor's words.

"I think, I'd rather it were not published," he said in a low voice. He kept his eyes fastened upon the floor; his face was very pale, with a bright spot of red in each cheek. "You see, too, it might not be successful. Then always afterward, I should have those other thoughts intruding."

"I believe, gentlemen, it would be a false step," the Professor continued. "This girl's character, her very being, is dependent now upon the thoughts we have of her, as up till now she is only a thought-girl. We want to keep her image pure, unsullied; the perfect image that Mr. Bates has created of her must remain unchanged. It would seem obvious, therefore, that we must be careful in the selection of the minds we use."

"What do you suggest?" the Banker asked.

"I believe it entirely feasible," the Professor answered, "for us to gather, here in this club, on some evening we may select, a large number of men whose minds are of the caliber we desire. There are hundreds such in New York City and its vicinity. Many of them are members of this club. These men, savants, let us call them," the Professor smiled, "unquestionably will assemble at our request for such a purpose. From one aspect, this is purely a matter of science, gentlemen, and in the most scientific way possible we must handle it. The trained minds of these men will enable them to direct their thoughts in whatever channels we suggest. The power of a hundred such mentalities will be greater than countless thousands chosen at random. We may be sure that nothing will creep into their mental pictures that we would not care to have there."

"Why not make up a tentative list now," the Doctor suggested, producing a lead pencil and an envelope from his pocket.

"I'll tell you who you want to get." The Playwright named a man from whose brain had sprung many of the most wonderful inventions of the age, a man whose name was known in every quarter of the globe. "He lives right over there in Jersey. Get him. A brain like that for concentration—good Lord!"

"He, of course," the Professor agreed, and the Doctor jotted down the name.

"How many do we need?" asked the Big Business Man, drawing his chair up beside the Professor.

"Lord, I'm hungry," the Banker announced suddenly, looking at his watch. "Eleven-thirty. No wonder. Say, gentlemen, before you get too deep into that, why wouldn't it be a good idea to get something to eat? Making up that list is going to be a long job. You'll have to go at it with system; you'll need twice as many names as the men you'll actually get."

The Playwright verified the time with astonishment.

"I had no idea it was so late. The main restaurant closes at ten, Sundays."

"We'll have a cold supper served up here," said the Banker. He turned to the Very Young Man. "Phone downstairs for a waiter, will you, boy? And have some writing paper sent up. They can't write many names on that miserable little envelope."

While the supper was being prepared, the Professor, the Doctor, and the Big Business Man continued making up the list of noted, learned men they thought might be available. They soon found the Banker was right—they would have to go about it systematically. With the name of the world-famous inventor standing at the head of the list, they followed with other names of hardly lesser note; men whose genius for invention had revolutionized the world. Then, with careful thought, they itemized all the various other branches of learning, making notes of such men as stood unquestionably at the head of their profession; and in particular they selected men whose original thought and research work gave certain, undeniable evidence of a strong, keen, powerful brain.

The Playwright engaged the Banker in a conversation aside, and occasionally they would make some suggestion to the three who were compiling the list.

"You want some of these well-known spiritualist mediums," the Playwright volunteered once.

This suggestion the Professor emphatically vetoed.

"This is purely a matter of science, gentlemen. We must

keep that always in mind. It has absolutely nothing to do with spiritualism, absolutely nothing. We must not confuse the two."

The list grew rapidly. To the names of the inventors they added several doctors, whose work in medicine gave evidence of a highly developed brain power. Then they discussed the members of the faculties of the several universities within a few hundred miles of New York. From these, they selected several professors of psychology—men of National fame. The departments of chemistry, astronomy, and others yielded still more names.

"One of those colleges has a department of Original Research," said the Big Business Man. "That's the sort of men we want, too."

The Professor knew of several such workers and their names were added.

"It seems to me," the Banker broke in at this point, "you needn't give the pedagogues all the credit for intellect. What about the financiers?" He named one of the greatest captains of industry, a financial giant, whose brain, like some gigantic magnet, had drawn to him great wealth and fame.

"I agree with you there," said the Professor heartily. "Men like that, while they know nothing, perhaps, of science, beyond any question have developed the power of concentration to a very high degree. They are accustomed to facing and solving unaided very big problems, else they could not have done what they have done. We want that type of brain, by all means."

THE DISCUSSION CONTINUED during the light supper that was soon served. Neither Guy Bates nor the Very

Young Man seemed inclined to eat much and soon left the table, sitting apart on opposite sides of the room, each apparently deep in his own thoughts. Finally, the Very Young Man rose, and crossing the room drew up a chair beside Guy.

"I've been thinking about that invention of yours," he began earnestly, as Guy looked up and smiled at him. "You didn't tell us very much about it, you know."

"There isn't much to tell," Guy answered. "I've made almost no headway with it."

"I was thinking, suppose you were able to work it out, just suppose you had it right here now," the Very Young Man balanced an invisible box on his knee, "could you make much money out of it?"

Guy smiled again, a little ruefully.

"If I had it, yes; I might easily get to be the richest man in the world. But I haven't got it, and, I'm afraid, I'm not likely to get it. Why?"

The Very Young Man leaned forward.

"Tell me all you know about it, please," he pleaded eagerly. "I've a reason—I—" Guy told him, and the Very Young Man listened with an absorbed attentiveness, an apprehension, almost, as though he feared some minutest detail would escape his understanding.

"Why do you ask all this?" Guy finished.

The Very Young Man relaxed.

"I was just thinking—nothing—only, suppose you did have it? Would you need much capital to develop it?"

"I've been promised unlimited capital. That part's nothing. But why do you ask me all this?"

The Very Young Man hesitated, then evinced a sudden

interest in the discussion that was still going on around the center table.

"They're getting that list pretty near finished," he said. "Gosh, I do hope it goes through all right."

The Banker for the moment seemed to be the center of the argument.

"Those are pretty big names," he was saying. "You can't get any bigger in this country. How do we know they're going to lend themselves to such a project as this?"

"They will," said the Doctor with conviction.

"I am confident they will," the Professor agreed. "You must understand, gentlemen, this affair is now really an extraordinary, a very big, experiment in scientific research. It has progressed far beyond the realms of mere theoretical discussion. Three hours ago, when we were merely talking theories, I would not for an instant have countenanced such a proposition as this proposed appeal to these men.

"But, gentlemen, don't you understand, that since that time we have established a fact, not a theory, a scientific fact. We created that girl; she has been here in this room tonight. Because her stay here was temporary makes it no less fundamentally a fact that she was here. But what we have already contributed to scientific knowledge is nothing compared to what we may be able to contribute with their assistance. They will come, I am convinced, if we approach them properly."

"How long should it take us to get them together?" the Big Business Man asked.

"A few days should be enough." The Professor looked around the table quietly; the Very Young Man got up and joined the group.

"We must plan this carefully, gentleman; we must make no mistakes in our presentation of the facts to these great men; we must neglect nothing that will aid us in making them respond to our appeal. It will not take long. Sunday should be a good night." The Professor paused an instant.

"I propose, gentlemen, that we formulate now, in detail, our plans, and that we put them into prompt execution tomorrow, to the end that at this hour next Sunday evening, we shall have assembled, in the restaurant downstairs, this gathering of men who represent the greatest power of intellect that America can produce. And with that power, gentlemen, I hope, I really believe, we shall be able to create permanently, as permanent human life ever is, this thought-girl we have all seen here in this room tonight."

AT TEN-THIRTY, THE following Sunday evening, the large restaurant that occupies the top floor of the Scientific Club was empty, save for the nimble waiters moving about, arranging its tables and chairs as though some huge banquet were being prepared.

By eleven o'clock, men began arriving; at first singly, or in couples, then in little groups with the rising of each elevator, presenting the tiny printed cards bearing their names that gave them instant entrance to the guarded room.

Inside, they walked idly about, smoking, greeting acquaintances and friends, gathering in little knots, discussing with lowered voices the experiment in which they had been asked to participate; or sat down some of them at one of the four long tables that had been placed in the room.

By eleven-thirty, there were several hundred men seated around the tables and only an occasional late-comer was arriving. There was in this gathering almost every possible type of man, physically. Some seemed hardly more than boys, smooth-shaven, well set up, alert-looking. Some were far past middle age, dignified, reserved, pedantic even, yet smiling frequently, with a boyish smile they had never lost, and mingling thus among their own kind, unbending with a freedom of speech that had in it nothing of the austerity with which one instinctively invests the savant.

At first glance, such a gathering might have appeared representative of any New York club's informal dinner, informal obviously, for most of the men were dressed in the clothes of their ordinary daily occupations. Yet upon closer inspection, no onlooker could have received that impression, for there was about every one of these men as they sat there, a peculiar radiation of personality, a pervading sense of repressed dynamic power. No austerity of mien betrayed its presence, no aloofness of manner betokened a consciousness of superiority. This assemblage of the truly great seemed to have no need for a simulation of greatness.

At eleven o'clock, when the men began to assemble in the restaurant room, the roof above was unoccupied, except by the lone figure of Guy Bates, sitting motionless on a little white stone bench in a corner of the garden. Presently, another figure, the figure of the Very Young Man, appeared at the top of the steps that led down into the hallway beside the restaurant below. It stood motionless a moment and then came swiftly across in the moonlight.

"You're here," said the Very Young Man, sitting down on the bench. "I wondered where you were."

Guy raised his head from his hands, blinking a little confusedly, like one who has been asleep.

"They're beginning to come in," the Very Young Man went on. "There'll be an awful lot of them. It's going to be all right."

Guy sighed, gazing abstractedly out over the rooftops of the city.

"Aren't you coming down? Come on, they'll all want to see you." The Very Young Man put an arm across his friend's shoulder. "You must be down there, you know, when it—it happens."

Guy's face showed very pale in the moonlight. His eyes were glistening; his lips trembled.

"I'm not going down"; he spoke so low the Very Young Man instinctively leaned forward, although in the hush of the garden his voice was plainly audible. "I—I can't go down there—until it's over—one way or the other."

"Oh," the Very Young Man was timidly disappointed and sympathetic.

"You understand, don't you? I just want to stay up here alone, until it's over, one way or the other."

The Very Young Man said nothing.

"I told Frank," Guy was almost whispering now, "and he'll explain it to them if they ask for me. I just want to sit up here alone. Maybe you'll let me know if—if anything happens."

The Very Young Man was upon his feet instantly. "Gosh, you bet I will," he cried. "Have you got the right time? They're going to begin it exactly at twelve, you know."

They compared the times of their watches.

"Eleven-fourteen now," said the Very Young Man. "I'll be going down. You'll surely think of her at twelve, won't you?"

The shadow of a smile hovered on Guy's lips, then faded.

"I'll be thinking of her—at twelve," he said soberly.

The Very Young Man hesitated, seeming reluctant to leave.

"I was wondering, it occurred to me—that—that while you were thinking of her—if maybe wouldn't it be a good idea to—to—think about—" He stopped, staring at the ground, the point of one shoe kicking up the white gravel.

Guy turned his head inquiringly; the Very Young Man looked up suddenly and met his questioning eyes.

"They'll be wanting me downstairs, maybe," he said abruptly, with the air of one who has reached a sudden decision. "I'll go down now, I guess. There might be something they wanted me to do. I'll let you know, after twelve, you bet."

He waved his hand with an awkward, embarrassed gesture, and turning swiftly, hastened back across the garden, leaving Guy sitting motionless upon the bench in the moonlight, chin in hand, staring out across the city.

WHEN THE VERY Young Man got back to the assembly-room he found that the gathering had increased. Only a few of the men were sitting at the tables as yet, most were moving slowly about the room, or standing in scattered groups, conversing. Threading his way among them, he spied three of his friends, the Professor, Doctor, and Big Business Man, standing together.

"I've been talking to Guy," he said as he approached. "He's up on the roof; he says, he won't come down; he wants to be alone."

"I'm a little sorry about that," the Professor said thoughtfully. "But naturally, Frank, from what you say," his grave glance rested on the Doctor a moment, "we must understand his feelings and respect them. It adds a complication, however, that I had not foreseen. You see, even with the tremendous intellectual power we shall undoubtedly be able to wield from this room," his eyes roved about over the rapidly gathering crowd, "I cannot conceive but that the greatest single force of all, perhaps even more than half of the total amount will emanate from the brain of Guy Bates.

"What may happen with this division of our forces, I cannot say. Perhaps, it will make no difference; there is, perhaps, no reason why it should, whether he remains in this room or in the garden up there. I believe we shall accomplish this materialization tonight. It may occur down here, but with him above it may not. That is a detail, unimportant if only we achieve the result. I should prefer though, that he were here."

"I told him all that," said the Doctor. "He understands, but he just cannot bring himself to come down. He is very overwrought. He cannot bring himself to face these strangers at such a time. He wants to be alone, up there. Under the circumstances, I feel that we should not urge him unduly."

The Very Young Man stood beside them a moment more, hesitating evidently upon the verge of saying something else. He waited until there was a pause in their conversation and then, plucking up his courage and addressing the Professor, he began,

"I've been thinking, Professor Hartwell—you know about that invention of Guy's—" He stopped, and then went on with a rush. "That's important, too, you know. If he's going to get this girl, he ought to have all the money

the invention would give him. And I've been thinking—I
tried to suggest it to him just now, but I was afraid to—it
seems to me that, maybe, if we had all these men thinking about the invention as well as the girl—that maybe,
we could get it, too. That would be great if we could do it,
wouldn't it? I thought, perhaps, you would suggest it to
them after a while, when they all get here." He paused,
breathless.

"I think, decidedly, that would be an error of judgment,"
said the Professor emphatically.

The Very Young Man's eager look faded to disappoint-
ment at the words.

"I am sorry, I cannot agree with you. I appreciate your
enthusiasm, and undoubtedly the materialization of the
invention, also, is to be desired."

"It would be a tremendous thing for the world," the
Very Young Man pursued earnestly. "You said it would, Dr.
Adams; you remember you told us it would."

The Professor continued.

"The success of this experiment means an extraordinary advance to science. We have gathered these scientific
men together for a certain purpose, to the achievement of
which we must bend every effort. The result to science will
be nearly as great if we succeed in the transmutation of this
girl as if we bring also the invention into material being.
We have already succeeded partially in materializing the
girl. That is a fact, and it is upon the evidence of the fact
these men of science are assembling. We have no means
of knowing what will happen with the introduction of the
other element; nothing there but pure theory to guide us.
We might defeat our main purpose. I have thought about

this point very seriously for several days. It would be a mistake to introduce it."

The Very Young Man looked at the Big Business Man and the Doctor, and seeing nothing in their faces to give him the least encouragement, he dropped the matter. A moment more, he lingered beside them, and then, watching his opportunity, slipped away unobtrusively.

Across the room, he saw the Playwright and the Banker standing together. He joined them swiftly.

"Good idea, boy," said the Banker approvingly, when the Very Young Man had sketched with hasty words his plan. "Anybody who neglects money is a fool. We all ought to've thought of that."

"Professor Hartwell says no," supplemented the Very Young Man, easing his conscience by concealing nothing. "He says it would be a bad plan to try it."

"It sounds all right to me," said the Playwright. "Great Scott, just suppose we did get them both!"

The Very Young Man looked at them intently; his face was flushed and eager. "I was just thinking—even if Professor Hartwell won't announce it—why can't we get some of them to try it anyway. You know lots of them personally, don't you?"

"Some," said the Banker. He caught the eye of a friend nearby and waved his hand. "I'll tackle 'em. Why not? It'll appeal to my friends all right."

The Playwright also agreed he would help.

"I'll tackle them, whether I know them or not," the Very Young Man added stoutly. "Who's the biggest of the bunch? I'll get him first."

The Playwright pointed to a small table nearby at which

six or eight men were seated, and named the name of an inventor who stands preëminent among the scientists of the world; an unassuming, unpretending, democratic American, a man of the people, with whom kings and emperors are proud to talk.

"You get him," said the Playwright, "and you've got with you the greatest mind in the world. The gray-haired one, see? That's his son beside him."

The Very Young Man scurried away without another word.

A few feet away from the table he paused, standing unnoticed in the crowd. The man the Playwright had pointed out, the Very Young Man had always known him by reputation, was plainly visible from where he stood. He was sitting low down in his chair. He was not in evening dress and the Very Young Man's first thought was that the collar of his coat hunched up rather awkwardly in the back. He was a man about seventy, smooth shaven, with a figure a little inclined to stoutness. His gray hair was thin, but long and scraggly, and just now a little tousled. He wore a loose, stand-up collar open at the throat, and a long, narrow black bow tie. But what the Very Young Man noticed particularly about him was his head. It didn't seem abnormally big and yet it obviously was large, large in a powerful, dominating way. The Very Young Man found himself thinking of a lion; perhaps, it was the set of his head, the heavy jaw; a lion sitting calm and placid now, but whose anger, once aroused, would cause the stoutest heart to quail.

He was, for the moment, sitting motionless, taking no apparent interest in the scene around him. Yet there was in his attitude nothing of somnolence, not a suggestion of apathy, or even stolidity. The Very Young Man could imagine readily that his thoughts were far distant, but wherever they were, he felt sure they were active, restless, searching. For all his physical inactivity, the Very Young Man thought this the most alert person he had ever seen.

The inventor's son sat beside him with his back partially turned, talking to the men next to him. He was seemingly a few years older than the Very Young Man, well dressed in a neat business suit, and with something of his father's look, mingled with an air of suavity, of graceful social polish, that was totally lacking in his father.

The Very Young Man, after a moment, started toward the table. His heart was beating wildly; he felt as if he were smothering. He hoped he was outwardly calm; he forced himself to walk slowly. He knew he wanted to speak to the inventor's son and with his growing trepidation decided resolutely to accost the great man himself.

With alarming abruptness, he found himself standing at the great inventor's elbow. A boldness born of timidity made him put his hand upon it as it lay on the arm of the chair.

"I'm one of the ones who was mixed up in that first experiment," he said; his voice sounded unfamiliar to him, as though someone else were speaking.

The great inventor shoved his chair back violently, and looked up over his shoulder; the Very Young Man felt a look that seemed to bore into the innermost hidden recesses of his mind.

"Eh?" said the inventor sharply. His voice was pitched overly loud and had a thin, nasal quality; the Very Young Man realized at once his hearing was defective.

"I was mixed up in that—I was one of the ones in that first experiment," the Very Young Man repeated in confusion, raising his voice a little. "I helped get the girl before. There's something I want to say to you, sir."

The inventor's eyes twinkled, his mouth expanded into a smile; the Very Young Man felt his soul basking in the warmth of the great man's genial mood.

"Good boy. Say it." His gesture made the Very Young Man bend lower until his mouth was close beside the great shaggy head.

"I've got an idea," the Very Young Man felt his timidity slipping from him, "about what we ought to do tonight. I want to tell you, sir."

The inventor's smile widened.

"Oh you have? Good boy. What is it?"

"It's about an invention—up there in that other world— with the girl." Instinctively, the Very Young Man found himself using short phrases of speech, as one does in speaking to the deaf.

"About an invention?" The great man chuckled. Then abruptly he turned around, gripping his son's arm. "Tell it to him," he said to the Very Young Man. He returned to his abstracted manner as though the Very Young Man had suddenly become non-existent.

To the inventor's attentive son, the Very Young Man told his theory, swiftly but in detail. When he had finished, the son transmitted it to his father with a clarity of speech and a succinctness born of long practice. The inventor listened closely, but impatiently, as though even with this compactness, this brevity, the ideas did not come fast enough. He was smiling again, nodding his head frequently, and occasionally muttering emphatic ejaculations to himself.

Before his son had finished, the inventor interrupted.

"That's all right. There's nothing the matter with that." He chuckled again.

"Professor Hartwell is against it," the inventor's son concluded immediately, giving his father all the data at hand.

"Oh, he is?" The inventor leaned toward the Very Young Man. "These college people think they know it all, don't they, boy? Well, we don't mind that, do we?" The Very Young Man felt himself standing in exaltation upon the very pinnacle of greatness, fraternally sharing it, arm in arm, with genius. "They think they know all about everything. We'll show 'em. Tell me all you know about that invention, boy."

The Very Young Man told him, as briefly, as clearly as he could, everything Guy had said. He was glad he had been so careful to make sure of understanding roughly.

The great inventor kept on nodding his head and chuckling gleefully. Before he was half finished the Very Young Man seemed to feel that already this wonderful man had grasped its intricacies as no one else had ever grasped them.

"All right, boy; that's enough," the inventor interrupted suddenly. A great weight fell from the Very Young Man's mind, a sense of relief, almost of exaltation, came to him. He felt as though the mystery of this invention, in which he was so interested, had somehow been suddenly miraculously solved.

The great inventor turned again to his son, and pointed to several men sitting nearby.

"I want to see them. Tell them to come over here."

The inventor's son rose and stood beside the Very Young Man.

"He'll probably do what you want," he said, and the Very Young Man felt himself dismissed.

He stood hesitating a moment longer beside the table. The great inventor evidently was again entirely oblivious to his existence. He wondered if he should say, "Thank you," and excuse himself, and immediately decided he wouldn't. Then, remembering he should see others of the men and win them to his plan, and that the time he had in which to do it was growing short, he turned and walked away, tingling all over with the variety of emotions the interview had left with him.

BY QUARTER OF twelve, there were no more of the men arriving. The room was crowded with them now, four hundred and fifty, perhaps. Most of them sat at the tables, but many still stood, or walked about. At ten minutes of twelve, there was a large clock-face at one end of the room, plainly visible, the Professor mounted a little platform set at the side, against one wall, where during the dinner hour a small orchestra played.

At the sound of the Professor's raised voice, a sudden hush fell over the room; then, at his direction, all of the men found chairs. In a moment more, the shuffle of their feet had died away; the room was silent, far more silent even than the darkened auditorium of an opera house.

"Gentlemen," began the Professor quietly, "I have but little time to address you," he spoke hardly above an ordinary conversational tone, "and yet I think, perhaps, there has been hardly anything left for me to say. No words of mine could add anything to the earnestness with which I can appreciate each one of you undertakes this experiment; so that, important as it is, I shall pass that aspect entirely.

"At twelve o'clock, gentlemen," he glanced at the clock-face, "precisely nine minutes from now, we shall dim the lights in this room, although not sufficiently to make it difficult for you to refer to the notes you have made if you should at any time desire to do so.

"I understand that each one of you has already conceived a mental image of this girl as we wish her to materialize tonight. Her face, her form, her general demeanor, her raiment; we have all agreed upon, and you each have detailed memoranda describing it. The importance of a uniform image, and its continuous, uninterrupted vividness in every mind, I need not emphasize. In the event of there being no resultant phenomena, the experiment will continue until twelve-fifteen, at which time the lights will be brightened."

He paused, and, looking down, met the eyes of a man sitting near the platform. "Only one other point, gentlemen," he resumed. "I have been in conference with the chairman and several members of the committee of investigation you have appointed. I agree with you absolutely upon that phase of the matter. If you will remember, in my first communication to each of you, I mentioned that we wished this affair kept, for the moment at least, from general publicity.

"You have my positive assurance, gentlemen, that no matter what may occur tonight, nothing of it will become known to the outside world until after your committee shall have made its careful investigation into the facts established. Even then, it will only be announced in the usual way, through the accustomed channels of scientific reports, and entirely at the discretion of, and in such form as, your committee directs.

"I can appreciate, naturally, that you gentlemen cannot lend your names to an undertaking such as this, unless it is handled in a thoroughly scientific and ethical manner and its results subjected to the most rigid scientific investigation. Upon that point, gentlemen, you have my word that your wishes will be respected."

Amid dead silence, the Professor stepped from the platform and sat down at one of the tables. After a moment, a hum of scattered conversation arose, a very restrained little hum, for every eye was fixed expectantly upon the clock.

At one minute of twelve all conversation had ceased. The men sat motionless, none of them looking at the clock now. Some were hunched low down in their chairs, others sat bolt upright and rigid. Still others leaned forward with elbows upon the table, chin in hand. Occasionally, one would move slightly, or glance hurriedly at a little white slip of paper. More than four hundred men there were, sitting close together; and yet each of them seemed absolutely detached from all his fellows, isolating himself mentally in a solitude as complete as though he were alone in the room.

The huge hands of the clock pointed to twelve, and the lights dimmed slowly. The hush in the room seemed to grow more intense; the pulse of the city outside, plainly audible now, throbbed against the shrouded windows like some gigantic, muffled heartbeat. The silence that hung about the motionless figures of the men grew deeper, heavier.

And through the lengthening minutes, the clock-hands jerked forward, unheeded.

ON THE ROOF above, Guy Bates still sat alone upon the little white stone bench in a corner of the garden. The stars were studded thick in the blue dome above and a huge, lazy moon hung low, its lengthening shadows streaking with black the golden-silver of its light in the garden. Beside him stood the shrouded recess of a trellised pergola; the heavy scent of its flowers seemed to enfold him like a cloak. In front, spread the rooftops of the city; some dark and silent, with brooding chimneys and the grotesque, ponderous bodies of water tanks set upon spindly legs; others, gaily hung with rows of dangling electric lights, the hotel roof-gardens where he could imagine care-free, joyous crowds of diners were assembled; and here and there above the roofs, a few of the higher office buildings towered grim and dominant, black silhouettes against the sky.

The soft, gentle breath of a summer night breeze fanned his cheek; he could hear it stirring and whispering in the flowered pergola beside him. He paid no heed to the passage of time. He tried to still his quickening pulse; he stared out over the city, or up into the twinkling sky, striving to pierce with his gaze the unfathomable distances beyond the stars; and always before him, hovered the image of a little, white, oval, girlish face with big, dark, pleading eyes that were fixed on his.

Abruptly, he sensed a sudden hush beneath him; he pulled out his watch with trembling hand, holding it close to his face in the pale moonlight. Then, shivering as though with a sudden chill, he hastily put the watch back into his pocket.

His brain was tired and confused. His legs were stiff and cramped; he shifted his feet uneasily over the white gravel beneath him. He remembered vaguely he had felt that way beside the waterfall of the little stream in Texas. She had stood there with him on the bank; her head, with the wistful little face, dark-framed by the flowing hair, had hardly reached his shoulder.

He remembered how her eyes looked that night, tender and yearning, and sorrowful; and how, too, they had looked that morning in Chicago, when with him she had sat upon the bed, watching the surf rise out of the lake—eyes tender and sweet and always sorrowful, patiently sorrowful. They had looked differently, he remembered, in the Realm of Unthought Things, in that brief little instant when they had stood together in the shadowed recess, and she had shown him his invention. Eager eyes they were then, tender, too, but sparkling with eagerness and pleasure. He remembered how she had held the little box in her hand, withholding it gently from him; that little box that held the invention he was someday to give the world. Then she had lifted the cover, unfolding its mysteries to his gaze. Parts of it had been missing there, he remembered, the parts of which he had already thought. They were clear in his mind now, those parts he had conceived so many years ago.

She had been very beautiful then. He thought that of all the times he had seen her, she had been most beautiful that moment, with her eyes dancing and the smile upon her lips while she showed him his treasure.

He remembered how a corner of the box, as she lifted it

up, had caught in the folds of her white flowing robe. She so often wore that robe; he remembered how very black her hair looked against its spotless white. Her hair was always down; even, when in the dress of a Texan girl, he had thought of her riding with him through the hills, she had worn it in looped braids that almost swept the saddle. He found himself wondering how she would look with it coiled upon her head, a great mass of hair crowning with black the rose-pinkness of her face. In evening dress, too— she would be very beautiful in that; a dress long and black and clinging to make of her slender little body a figure graceful and queenly. Perhaps, just a single red rose at her breast, to match the redness of her lips.

He had never seen her in evening dress. How white her shoulders gleamed above the black of the satin, and her hair piled 'round and 'round on her head.

He had often seen girls dressed like that, sometimes even right here in the roof-garden of the Scientific Club, but never could one look so beautiful as she. He wondered how it would seem to see her standing over there in the shadows by the wall. Breast-high to her, that low wall of stone; as she leaned against it, he feared it might crush the single red rose she wore.

A rose to match her lips. He was glad when she turned to face him, to see it was still there, unhurt, against the soft folds of her dress. Her face seemed very pale in the light of the waning moon; but there was color in it, too, the delicate pink of health and youth. Her big dark eyes were fixed on his, eyes melting with tenderness, with infinite tenderness. The look of sorrow in them seemed to be gone now; another light shone in its place, a light of eagerness, a sparkle of joy. They had looked just like that, he thought, when she had shown him his invention; and now he noticed, as she stood there, leaning forward, she was holding a little box in the crook of her arm.

A long shadow from the trellis bordering the path fell across her figure; the black of her dress seemed to melt into it, all vague and indistinct, as though almost she were not standing upon the ground at all. Then she began walking toward him, along the path, and as she came out into a patch of moonlight, he saw plainly the twinkle of her little silver slippers as she walked. He held his breath, and then clearly, unmistakably, he heard the soft crunch of her heels in the gravel of the path.

A church bell down in the city began chiming the quarter hour. Guy leaped to his feet.

"You!" he cried. "Then you did come; they did succeed after all!" The sudden realization that swept over him made him tremble violently; he put a hand against the pergola to steady himself.

The girl stopped in the middle of the path, only a few feet from him. He saw her figure sway, and the box slip from her arm and fall to the gravel path; the noise of it sounded startlingly loud in the silence of the garden. She stooped, but Guy reached it before her, picking it up, feeling it solid and heavy in his hands. He met her eyes as he straightened, eyes that he saw were tired, very tired, but shining with love and with happiness.

"You see, I brought it to you," she said and his ears heard the vibrant, physical voice of a human girl. "You have it now, in your hands at last, what you have always wanted."

He set the box down on the stone bench mechanically,

his mind in a daze. The girl had followed him forward and stood again at his side, a slender, graceful girl-woman, in a long black evening gown, with a single red rose at her breast and her glorious black hair piled high upon her head. Her exquisitely lovely, sensitive little face was upturned to his; the eyes that he saw were shining with a woman's love, a soft, steady, glowing light that made them transcendently beautiful.

"You have brought me here," she said softly. "You— and all those others. It has been very hard, waiting all the years. And tonight it was very hard, too, coming." The shy, wistful look he knew so well came back to her eyes as she added. "I'm here, Guy." Her fingers plucked a flower from the arbor beside them, toyed with it idly a moment, then tossed it away. "I'm here. Didn't you—I mean, Guy, aren't you glad I'm here?"

The little note of archness in her voice, like some swift-acting reagent, clarified his thoughts; the turgid pool of his mind became clear as a crystal spring; his confusion, his doubts, vanished. With full realization, came a sudden flood of tenderness. He stooped and gathered her almost roughly into his arms. He could feel the warmth of her flesh where his hand touched her shoulder; he heard her frightened heart beating against his.

A dark, silent figure appeared in the garden at the head of the stairs; it hesitated an instant and then ducked back out of sight. A moment afterward the faint tones of the Very Young Man's voice floated upward.

"She's here! She's come! She's up there now with him."

There was a brief silence, and then came the sound of

many shuffling feet, and shouts, a faint clapping of hands, and a muffled, scattered cheering.

Guy released the girl abruptly. She stood silent, breathing fast, her face flushed, her long black lashes lowered.

"They'll want to see you down there," he said gently, "those men who have helped us tonight."

He stooped and picked up the box, holding it under his arm. As he turned back to her, he saw a crowd of figures surging up into the garden, and halting, undecided, near the top of the stairs.

"They'll want to see this, too," he said. "Our contribution, yours and mine, to the science of your new world. Will you go down now, dear?"

She lifted her lashes and met his gaze unwavering.

"I will, of course, it you wish it," she answered simply.

THE OTHER ROAD

1

"GENTLEMEN, I ASKED Dr. Adams to bring me here among you tonight for one specific, selfish purpose. It is that I may perform this unusual experiment upon myself here, now, with your knowledge and your help."

His listeners leaned forward expectantly but no one spoke as he paused. The light from the single electrolier over the big center table plainly showed his figure. He was tall and lean—a man something under forty. His brown, wavy hair was noticeably gray at the temples. His eyes were gray, piercing at times, and wistful in his more contemplative moods. His smooth-shaven face was rugged of feature, and yet in its thinness carried an expression of spirituality a little at variance with its strength. He was the only man in the room not in evening dress.

"I say my wish is entirely selfish, gentlemen," he went on. "And yet, perhaps, that is not strictly so. My case may have some scientific value. That was my only excuse for suggesting to Dr. Adams," he indicated the Doctor as he spoke, "that I make the experiment here at the Scientific Club." He paused again.

"In the exact sense of the word," said the Banker, "I wouldn't say there was a scientist in the room."

The Doctor put in quickly.

"I wanted this first experiment to be done most informally. Mr. Davis has no idea, as yet, to what it may lead, or in what is its scientific value. It is purely a personal matter with him. I selected you gentlemen because, well, because we are all such close friends—we all understand each other, we are sympathetic—and discreet."

The Very Young Man deprecatingly looked his appreciation.

The Big Business Man picked up a little glass vial that lay on the table. "This powder you mentioned—"

"Is odorless, tasteless, soluble in water," said the visitor. He took the vial gently from the Big Business Man's hand, stared at it quizzically an instant, and replaced it on the table. "It does not look as potent as, I hope, it may prove to be." He smiled. "Yet gentlemen, I sincerely believe it to be the most remarkable drug ever compounded in the history of medicine!"

There was another short silence, broken by the Banker. "You have told us practically nothing so far," he said, "except that you wished to have us observe the effects upon you of taking some drug. I assume Dr. Adams knows—" He paused questioningly.

"It is rather a curious matter, gentlemen," said the Doctor. "I think Mr. Davis will explain his ideas to you. The experiment is very simple. He had, many years ago, the choice of two diametrically opposed courses. He had come to a vital fork in the road of his life. He regrets the decision he made, the road he took. You have all had similar experiences, no doubt. He wants to find out what might have been. He wants, by this experiment, to follow in his thoughts, his memories, this other road of his life—the road he could have taken, but did not."

The men considered this a moment.

"The other roads to our life," murmured the Big Business Man.

"Then this powder—" the Banker began finally.

"I think," interrupted the Doctor, "if Mr. Davis will do so, he had better tell you his story and his ideas in detail. Then I am sure you will understand. It is most interesting, gentlemen, whether you consider it scientifically or not." He looked expectantly at his friend.

MORTON DAVIS HESITATED.

"To be quite frank with you, gentlemen," he said finally, "I had intended to tell you very little." He raised his hand apologetically. "Dr. Adams knows all about it, of course. But the thing is so—shall I say intimate? so personal a matter, I have felt a natural reluctance to talk about it."

"If you could, Morton," interjected the Doctor. "I—these are very good, close friends of mine, as you know. They will understand, and make allowances, no matter what you say." He turned to the others. "You can understand, gentlemen," he went on. "There are some things about one's private life, thoughts, ideals, sentiment, perhaps, that a man does not talk of readily to other men. This affair intimately concerns such things, such feelings. I can appreciate how he—"

Morton Davis interrupted him.

"You are all very kind, gentlemen. I like your attitude. I—I really believe you should know exactly what is in my mind. I am going to tell you, plainly. I only hope," he smiled again his charming smile, "I do hope though, that in the telling, you will acquit me of being a silly, romantic, overgrown boy."

"We will," the Very Young Man burst out. "Of course, we will."

The others settled themselves more comfortably in their big leather chairs. Sympathy and expectancy were evident in the expression of each.

"I will go back eighteen years," began Morton Davis slowly. "Just eighteen, to a June day when I was a boy of twenty. I was engaged to be married then to a little blue-eyed, golden-haired girl. I—I know, in a boy's way, I loved her very much. She was the sweetest, dearest little thing in the world." He smiled a little embarassedly at the grave men who faced him attentively.

"I mention this particular day because on that day I reached the fork in the road of my life that Dr. Adams mentioned a few moments ago. We were to have been married, this little girl and I, within a few weeks. The date had already been set. Then we quarreled. The break was sudden, unexpected, and perhaps for that, seemingly more nearly irreparable. Harsh, vehement, angry words passed between us; the unreasoning quarrel of seventeen and twenty. In maturity, words spoken in the heat of anger are taken more lightly. How different things are in adolescence, gentlemen!

"I left her and went away, alone, that afternoon, to think it out. My anger had cooled; but there came no calmer reasoning. That is the pathetic part of it, gentlemen. There was nothing then in my heart but bitterness; and a great self-pity and a sense of martyrdom. My love seemed dimmed, sullied; my boyish ideals of her broken.

"I had come to a fork in the road of my life, although I did not reason it so then. I could have taken either path.

But I had no realization that my whole future happiness could be made or marred by my actions in that crisis. I only knew I was hurt, bruised, disillusioned.

"I went back to her that afternoon. I was very calm, dignified, cold. I stated my case, proved myself right. I even asked her for the ring, and facing about with my heart full of the self-pity of a martyr, left her in tears. It was many years before I saw her again."

He paused. The Very Young Man was leaning forward with his hands tightly clenched over his knees.

"And during those years, you—she—what happened?" he asked tensely.

The Big Business Man sighed. It was evident his feelings had been more deeply touched than the expression on his face showed.

"You did not forget her then," he said gently.

"I did not forget her, no. I went my way and tried to forget. With my family, I went to another city. Other girls drifted in and out of my life. But I never did forget. The vision of her persisted—a sort of longing for what might have been. It is that, I think, that has kept me from marrying all these years. And the longing grew stronger, more tangible, until finally I realized it was not the loss of an ideal I was mourning, but the loss of the girl herself. I knew then that I was still in love with her, more deeply in love than I had ever been. I regretted bitterly the mistake I had made; I decided to see her, to take up, if possible, our life where I had broken it off.

"Nearly five years had elapsed. I traveled a thousand miles to the city where she was. I did not go to see her, for my inquiries brought to light the fact that she had been married a year, that her first child had just been born.

"GENTLEMEN," MORTON DAVIS went on earnestly. "I suppose you think my story very trite. Doubtless, it is not particularly unusual; perhaps even one of you has had a somewhat similar experience, certainly you have read of them often. The thing was a shock to me, of course, but it did not wreck my life. I was still only twenty-five. Youth takes its tragedies lightly, even though self-pity may make them seem very terrible at the moment. I determined again to forget her. The world was full of girls, I reasoned. I went back home and took up the normal course of my life.

"But, gentlemen, I never married nor did I ever forget. The years passed. The memory of the girl grew dim with the haze of time. I was not morbid, not brooding over a lost love. Do I make that clear? I knew she was married, happily, so far as I could understand, living out her pre-ordained life just as I was living out mine. But always that shadowy other life, the life we might have had together seemed spread out before my consciousness.

"I am a chemist by profession. At first, I took a medical degree and began the practice of medicine." He smiled at his friend the Doctor. "Dr. Adams knows I soon decided it was a poor business; probably because I would have made a poor physician. I stopped it and became a chemist.

"Four years ago my business brought me permanently to New York, the city where she had been living all those years, where she still is living. One Sunday afternoon, a sudden impulse seized me. I knew her address; I called at her house to see her.

"Fourteen years had passed. I had grown to manhood.

The emotions of my adolescence had become only vague memories. There was hardly anything more in my mind that Sunday afternoon than a sentimental curiosity to see this girl who might once have become my wife.

"She chanced to admit me herself—she was alone in the apartment at the time. She knew me at once. I need not go into details of our agitation at the meeting. She led me into the living-room, and we talked, conventionally, of what had happened to us both all those years.

"She had changed very slightly. A little fuller of figure, perhaps, graver of face, and with a new poise of manner. But to my eyes she was the same little blue-eyed, golden-haired girl I had once expected to make my wife.

"For perhaps half an hour, we talked and established quite the basis of two old friends. But, gentlemen, a peculiar, very peculiar thing I want to make clear to you. My inner feelings, during the time we were talking there quietly together, were somehow uncanny. Can I make you understand that? A thousand truant thoughts kept surging through my head. I began to feel as though I were forcing myself to hold firm to realities; vague shadowy *impressions* (they were hardly more than that) seemed to crowd about us, obtrude into our conversation. I did not understand them then. I do now. They were not memories of the past we had each actually lived; they were the shadows of the life we *might have lived*, that other road, our life together that we had missed.

"The thing was quite unmistakable, gentlemen; intangible, but unmistakable. I grew progressively uneasy, harassed, almost; and I think she shared my feelings.

"I have said we established a basis of good friendship.

That was so at first. But gradually, I became aware that underneath still lay something deeper, something we had once had that remained unchanged. It was almost as though she still loved me, and I her. It would have been quite that, I think, except that mature, normal people cannot so easily, even in their thought, set aside the barriers of conventional life that have been raised between them.

"In the old days she used to sing for me, and I used to play the piano to accompany her. I asked her to sing now, there was a piano standing beside us, and she would not. Her husband did not care for music, she said; and she had not sung for many years. I had given her many little books of poetry in those old days. I remembered she had started a sort of scrap-book of poetical quotations that particularly appealed to her girlish fancy. We had memorized them together as she wrote them in.

"Something prompted me, incautiously, to recall that scrap-book to her that afternoon. Without a word, she went into an adjoining room and after a time laid it, and a few of the old songs I had loved to hear her sing, on my lap. It transpired then that her husband had never seen them—or at least did not understand the sentiment attached to them.

"For one brief moment she spoke of her husband almost as an outsider. Recovering herself, she flushed, and took the things back. But I caught a glimpse of tears trembling in her eyes. I know we were both a little frightened at the memories we had stirred.

"HER HUSBAND AND little daughter came in soon after that. The child was a fine, rosy-cheeked little girl of nine. It occurred to me then, as I made friends with her, to wonder how that other child, *my* child, would have looked. Would my little child have been so straight and sturdy as this? Would that other soul, that even now must be hovering out there Beyond, have shone from girlish eyes like these, if we had given it body?

"I made friends with the little girl at once. As she stood there between my knees, curiously fingering my scarf-pin, while I talked with her, I seemed suddenly to sense the existence of that other child. It was quite an indefinable feeling, gentlemen; and yet I must repeat, unmistakable. It was, shall I say? as though some dim little presence were hovering about us, an outsider striving with infinite pathos for recognition, for a share of the attention I was giving this rival.

"I met the mother's eyes. The curious, slumbering, brooding look that shone for an instant from their depths, made my heart leap. I do not know what was in her thoughts at that moment nor what *she* felt. I have never known. But I believe, firmly, sincerely, that she too sensed that yearning, wan little presence whose only real existence lay along that other road—the road we had not taken.

"I had talked with her husband for no more than five minutes when many more things became plain to me. He was a good-natured sort of chap, a man a few years older than I, bluff, hearty, one of the rough and ready type. His red, slightly heavy face, his thick neck, close-cut hair, and short bristling mustache, made me think, inevitably, of the conventional type of butcher. I mean that as no disparagement, gentlemen. He was obviously well-bred. I mention it merely to show that in appearance, and I realized afterward, in actuality, he was one of those men concerned entirely with material things. Obviously, he loved her, made her a good husband. A comfortable home, good food, clothes, servants, all those material comforts that money can bring, and a good-natured, comrady, kindliness of treatment—that was life and love and romance to him.

"The matter was very plain to me then, gentlemen, as I have said. The things that she and I had woven about our love, even at seventeen and twenty, *he* had never given her. And she had clung to the memories of them, never quite giving them up, even though she loved him as her husband, and was comfortably happy with her home and her maternal affection for her child.

"Do I make myself clear? You cannot deny romance to the heart, the spirit, that is capable of feeling it, capable of appreciation and understanding. You may substitute everything else, but that little spark of longing always remains. It will force nothing, do nothing drastic, but even though it never breaks out into flame, it will always go on glowing, to the end of life itself. They say that is essentially a feminine feeling, gentlemen, but I think not. I think it entirely concerns the individual, without regard to sex.

"I will be briefer. This scene I have described occurred four years ago, here in New York. I have been here ever since; they are still living in the same apartment, it is not more than two or three miles from where we are at the present moment, and I have seen her within a month.

"**SINCE THAT SUNDAY** afternoon four years ago, I have taken my place as an old friend of the family, a casual, somewhat infrequent visitor to their home. Once or twice I have entertained her husband at my club. Chance has seldom thrown me with her alone since that first meeting.

On the very few such occasions that have occurred, we have scrupulously talked of impersonal things, with only an occasional slip. But underneath our casual, commonplace intercourse, everything that I have tried to describe to you is lying. I am sure she feels it as strongly as I.

"Are we still in love with each other? I should hardly say that. It is scarcely so material a thing even as human love that binds us together now. Perhaps, it is a feeling I should characterize essentially as spiritual. I do not mean that tritely. To some natures, the spirit is a vague, incomprehensible thing, little more than a word to juggle with. To others, it is very real. It obtrudes constantly on the physical. Its hopes, fears, longings, and its love, are as recognizable to the individual as are their physical counterparts.

"We are bound together, she and I, by a potentiality that, could it find expression, might make life a thousand times more worthwhile for us both. Can you think then, that we have been tempted to step from the separate roads we are traveling? That is absurd. The longing of spirit has never found satisfaction in such a course. Lust of body, physical only, though sometimes masquerading as something higher, has done it since the beginning of time. But the soul is more patient. It hopes, and yearns, but waits, enduring all.

"There is, I think, in neither of our hearts, a discontent at our material existence. I know I accept things as they are. There is only that intense desire to know what might have been, and the growing perception of my senses to the lights and shadows along that other road. That is what has brought me here among you tonight."

Morton Davis stopped speaking. A sudden embarrassment at the intimate unreservedness of his words brought the blood to his lean face.

FOR A MOMENT, there was complete silence in the room. Then the Banker shifted his feet noisily on its polished floor, sat up in his chair, and picked up the little vial of white powder that lay on the table.

"Your story—we—the thing is understandable, I am sure." He looked around at his friends. He spoke almost gruffly, as though to avoid any possibility of sentiment in his manner. He turned the little vial about in his fingers questioningly. "What you have told us so far—this powder—I cannot say I quite see the connection."

"He will tell you about that," put in the Doctor. "Explain about the drug, Morton; what led you to compound it."

Morton Davis resumed. His manner still carried embarrassment, which, as he forgot himself in his narrative, gradually disappeared.

"For four years, gentlemen, ever since that Sunday afternoon, my mentality, you might call it my subconscious mind, has been acutely aware of that other, that secondary branch of my life. Perhaps, I have developed a super-sensitiveness. I suppose that is probable. It is now almost as though I had once actually lived that other life, forgotten it completely, and now the dim memories of if were coming back to me."

The Doctor interjected.

"Explain exactly what you mean, Morton. Tell them how you conceive those other roads we all have to our lives."

Morton Davis smiled earnestly.

"I think I can make it clear to you gentlemen, in a very few words. I conceive our life from birth to death, to be one direct road. That road we traverse from birth, until, at its very end, we come to our death. That is, let us say, the main road. It is the life we actually live, the life of which our five senses are thoroughly cognizant. Is that clear?"

He paused to receive the assent of his listeners, then went on.

"Now, I think you can understand, gentlemen, that in addition to that main road, that central stem, there are many diverging branches. These are our secondary lives, the lives we might have lived, the branching roads, any one of which we might have taken, but did not.

"I do not mean this figuratively, I mean that actually, in some way we cannot understand, these other roads to our life belong to us, are a part of us. They hover about just beyond the ordinary, dull perceptions of our senses. Perhaps, they are all lying hidden in our subconscious mind. I do not know.

"Some of these other roads are more vital than others. Some we came nearer taking, let me phrase it. A consciousness of those more important ones, the influence of them, is, perhaps, more readily felt.

"I have outlined how that one divergent path of my life has affected me. I have said my senses are perhaps over-acute—I have developed possibly a power, or a sensitiveness to such impressions, above normality. But gentlemen, do you think that you, yourselves, have throughout the course of your lives been entirely oblivious to such impressions? Think back a moment, each of you. Go back to some crisis, some big fork in the road of *your* life. If you *had* taken that other course, perhaps even the choice was involuntary, then *if* fate, or circumstances, or what you will, had forced you into that other road, what would your life have been?

"Have you never thought of that? Have you never felt regret at having taken a wrong course? In a daydream, perhaps, has your mentality never wandered out into that realm of things that might have been?"

Morton Davis's voice had risen to sudden power. He paused; then added:

"Is my case then, so different from your own?"

His hearers were startled by this abrupt challenge. The Very Young Man burst out with earnest eagerness,

"Oh, *I've* thought of such things, often."

"So have I, I suppose." The Big Business Man spoke as though striving carefully to voice his meaning. "Such conjectures, such dreams—I suppose everyone has them. But they—"

"But they are only dreams," the Banker finished.

Morton Davis smiled quietly.

"I think you have reached the crux of the whole matter there, gentlemen. I differ with you. I conceive them not to be dreams, most decidedly not."

THE BANKER STARTED to retort, then checked himself. The Big Business Man put in thoughtfully.

"Perhaps, that is because your conception of dreams differs from ours. For myself, I have never understood them. Who shall say what they are, from what they spring?"

"Let us not get into a discussion of the origin of dreams," said the Doctor. "That is—"

"What I meant by dreams—" the Banker began.

Morton Davis interrupted him earnestly.

"Let me explain further, gentlemen. I think I can make

it clear, it is so very clear to me. These thoughts of what might have been float through your mind. You consider them daydreams, merely idle conjectures, ephemeral, fleeting, mental whims of the moment. I do not. They are, to my understanding, secondary memories—definite, actual, unchangeable."

"What do you mean by *secondary* memories?" the Banker asked.

"Let us take, for example, one big fork in the road of your life," Morton Davis answered. "At that turning point, say twenty years ago, you had a God-given right of choice. You could have taken either road, the choice was yours, there is no denying that. The road you did take became your physical life. Therefore, naturally, it is the life of which your physical senses are cognizant. And as you travel along it, the memories of it as it passes remain with you. These let us call primary memories.

"But, gentlemen, merely because you did not turn your physical life into that other road when God gave you the choice, does not change or obliterate its potentialities. Inherently, it remains the same; you no longer have the physical choice of taking it, that is all. *Had* you taken it, the life you are living now would have continued to hold all *its* potentialities, but your physical senses would have been cognizant of the other: that is the only difference.

"In the cosmic scheme of things as God has created them, *you* can alter nothing. It is merely that from a multiplicity of potentialities which are assigned to you by the Creator, chance, and your mentality, make continual selection. What is chosen forms your physical life, which I call primary. But all that other, which you have disregarded, neglected, or avoided, remains as much your life as though you actually had lived it—and your memories of it are secondary. You cannot fail to realize, that, gentlemen. It is too obvious once you reason it out."

"Then this—these secondary memories—" the Banker began again.

"They are just like any other memories. Only instead of being the recollections of one part of your life, the physical, they are the memories of another—the part you *could* have lived in your physical being, but did not."

"*I* understand you now," cried the Very Young Man impulsively.

"The principal difference between ordinary memories and these other secondary memories," Morton Davis went on, "is that the latter come less frequently, less vividly, and generally with less continuity. I think that is very understandable. The perception of them depends, I should say, upon the higher qualities, perhaps the more spiritual qualities, of our being. But that every normal person is able to have, and does have, secondary as well as primary memories, I think there can be no question. Individuals differ, of course. One person's memory is keen; another's is dull. Thus too, one may have very keen secondary memories; another may not.

"But what is more important, gentlemen, what I want to make clear to you now, is that physical or mental environment of the moment may sharpen temporarily the individual's acuteness of perception to all memories. Physical languor, which can be induced, has its effect. Or a sudden derangement of the physical functions. They say a person being rendered unconscious under water has a brief, extraordinary keenness of memory. Or in illness—the medicine you take. Have they never given you something to quiet you, send you gently to sleep?"

He appealed to the Doctor.

"Valerian, for instance? A very simple drug, gentlemen. Have you never taken it, and then had yourself drift away on a quiet, placid stream of memories?"

"The point that you are making now, Morton," the Doctor interrupted, "I think you should explain to them, is that all memories, secondary as well as primary, can be influenced by changing our physical or mental condition, can be made more vivid. And that—"

The Banker jerked himself upright in his chair.

"Then this drug—"

"Will enormously increase, temporarily, my acuteness of perception of the secondary memories of my life," said Morton Davis quietly. "It is to test its workings that I came here among you this evening, as I have said.

"You can readily understand, gentlemen," he went on a little hastily, as though to avoid the comments or the sensation his last words might have created, "that when I came here this evening, it was with no wish or intention to speak so fully or so intimately of my personal affairs. I wished merely to have you, with Dr. Adams, help me in what we may term a scientific experiment; to have you note its progress and result, which I cannot do for myself, and which Dr. Adams preferred not to do alone. That I have gone into the matter so fully I think now, has been an advantage. You can understand it more thoroughly; the results we obtain will mean more to you now.

"TO WHAT I have already said, I need add little. You can

appreciate that since that Saturday afternoon four years ago, I have been steadily growing more and more acutely conscious of the memories of that one particular regretfully unchosen other road to my life. The thing has, gentlemen, in a word, become almost an obsession. For nearly three years I have been experimenting to bring myself to a more complete cognizance of the events that for me, and her, would have been along that other road; to enable me to remember that other part of my life more vividly, with more continuity, let me say:

"At first, I tried merely the mental—to bring into my mind by an effort of will, of concentration, the mental pictures for which I groped. Then my knowledge of medicine and chemistry led me to try influencing the mental, and perhaps the spiritual through the physical, by the use of medicine. I have indicated, I think, how that occurs to a limited extent with all of us. The final result of my experiments is that powder." He indicated the little vial on the table.

"Have you tested it out?" the Big Business Man asked. "What will it do?"

"I have tested the effect of many medicines, and of many combinations. I need not trouble you with technical details—Dr. Adams and I have been over all that. The final compound, which I have here, I have never tried in this exact form. But I know what I have to expect, although, gentlemen, I must confess, the results I have obtained have been gotten by the patient process of elimination rather than by any inductive reasoning. Dr. Adams and I can prognosticate to a degree *how* this powder will affect me, but—"

"Tell us how," the Very Young Man suggested.

"Wait a moment," cried the Banker. He was the oldest man in the room, and his suddenly alert manner seemed indicative of a desire to command the situation for the moment. "We've been all over this thing pretty thoroughly in a theoretical way. Now, let us get down to something practical. You propose to take this powder now?"

"Yes," said Morton Davis. "If you gentlemen agree that it is advisable."

"And under its influence your mentality will be subjected to a series of visions, of dreams?" The Banker raised both his thin little hands deprecatingly and smiled. "You will pardon me. I am so often sarcastic, they say, but this time I do not mean to be. I accept your own interpretation—your reasoning certainly is logical. These subconscious recollections, then, of what never did happen, but would have happened had your choice of life been different, they will come to you, and when the influence of the drug wears off you will repeat them to us? Do I understand that correctly?"

"No, George," interposed the Doctor, "not at all in that way. I do not understand that he will go into a comatose condition, a trance, or anything of that kind. *You* explain it, Morton."

"It is not unconsciousness," said Morton Davis. "It is more as though I were in dual personality. I shall remain conscious of the room here, shall be able to converse with you, answer your questions. At least, that is what I expect. But something of me will be detached, living back over that other life. I shall be conscious of that, too, as vividly, perhaps, as I am of you and this room."

"How can you select what you want to live over, what

memories you wish brought to you?" the Big Business Man asked.

"By my own effort of will. These will be to me no different from ordinary memories are to you. You can of your own volition think back to any period of your life within your memory, can you not?"

"Then you'll be able to think backward and forward in it," cried the Very Young Man. "You'll be able to pick out any part of it you please?"

"Yes," said Morton Davis. "Just that. I anticipate the same control over it that you have over the memories of your own physical life that is past. I shall select," he smiled a little wistfully, "naturally, I shall select that one other road of which we have been talking. I shall review it consecutively, just as you would review your own past life." He paused.

"I think, gentlemen," he added, "I think with your permission I shall make the experiment now. There is nothing more of value we can say. And of course you can appreciate," his voice seemed to take on a new note of gentleness, "it is only natural for me to be eager to know what is to be unfolded to me tonight."

THE DOCTOR ROSE to his feet; a sudden stir of anticipation communicated itself among the other men.

"There's some water here," said the Doctor. He dissolved a portion of the powder in half a glass of water and handed it to his friend.

"Are you going to turn down the lights, or what?" The Big Business Man's voice sounded just a little strained.

The Doctor switched off the side lights. The corners of the room were plunged in darkness. The only light now came from the center electrolier hooded above, and casting its beam directly downward upon the table. Most of the men were just outside its circle of illumination, in semi-darkness. Upon the figure of Morton Davis, sitting bolt upright in his chair with the glass in his hand, the light fell full.

"May we speak with you, ask you questions? Or will you just talk to us?" Unconsciously the Very Young Man had lowered his voice almost to a whisper.

"Let us all just act normal," said the Doctor. "Act just as though he were sitting there reviewing his past life in memory. He will tell us about it as the memories come to him; we can question him when we wish. There need be nothing mysterious, occult or weird about it at all."

There came another short, solemn pause; the Doctor seated himself. Morton Davis held the glass in untrembling hand; his eyes stared far away. Abruptly, he raised the glass to his lips and drank the liquid, replacing the glass on the table unhurriedly. Then he relaxed in his chair. His eyes did not close, but stared away into the distance; a smile curved upward the corners of his mouth.

AN OPPRESSIVE SILENCE fell over the little group.

"Why are you smiling, Morton?" the Doctor asked softly, after a moment.

Slowly, Morton Davis turned to face him. It was, almost, as though the question had aroused him from prolonged meditation. He answered quite in his normal voice, except that it had perhaps an added quality of abstraction, as the absent-minded person answers abstractedly when suddenly questioned.

"Why do you smile, Morton?" the Doctor repeated.

"I was smiling to think how easily young lovers become reconciled when they have quarreled. I remember how big, how serious, that quarrel looked. And how easily we straightened it but that afternoon."

The answer came so naturally, it was so rational, that it caused the greater surprise. The men exchanged glances, forcing themselves to smile. There was nothing in Morton Davis's manner, or in his voice, that was uncanny or even unreal. Yet each of his listeners knew that the reconciliation he mentioned had never occurred; and the knowledge made each of them solemn with that feeling of awe that comes with the presence of the Unknown.

The Doctor went on gently:

"Your life when you were first married—tell us about it."

"We were married in New York," Morton Davis answered. "After our honeymoon—" He stopped abruptly; there was a long silence broken only by the labored breathing of the Banker. Morton Davis sat relaxed in his chair, his eyes fixed idly on the floor. By his look, he might have been alone in the room, in deep and calm meditation. The Doctor cleared his throat nervously.

"After your honeymoon," he prompted.

Morton Davis's eyes swung up to his friend's face; he smiled again.

"One doesn't ever tell about one's honeymoon; that is supposed to be a secret, is it not? Afterward, we went to live in a little New Jersey village, the village of Sumner. I can remember so well that miserable little hotel we lived in while our house was building, and while I was taking my medical degree in the city. Dora hated that hotel. But we were happy, happy as only two young married people can be."

The Very Young Man whispered to the Doctor; the Doctor nodded his approval.

"Tell us about the home you built, Morton. Can you remember it so vividly? You realize now, do you not, that it does not exist except as the home you would have built, had you really chosen to live this other life?"

A shadow crossed Morton Davis's face; he started perceptibly.

"I—you—you remind me. Of course, I understand. I had forgotten." The realization seemed to pain him; the watching men could see him struggling with his emotion. He looked around at them a little vaguely. "Has anyone a cigarette? I—"

The Very Young Man hastened to supply him.

Morton Davis smoked a moment in silence.

"When one remembers such happy times as those, it is rather a shock, the realization that it is only what might have been."

"You started practicing medicine I suppose," the Doctor interposed, "soon after you had taken your degree?"

"Yes," said Morton Davis, "and it was hard going at first. My father had given us money to build the house and get along on until I was fairly at work. After that," he smiled reminiscently, "the struggles of a very young physician trying to get established in a new community—we know what that means, Doctor, do we not?

"But I made out. Gradually, my practice built up. But those first three years, that was tough going. Especially that third year, the year Dora—"

His voice trailed away. A look of pain, of sorrow, almost of terror came into his face. His hands gripped the arms of his chair tightly; his whole body tensed.

The watching men exchanged apprehensive glances, looking to the Doctor for explanation.

"What is it, Morton?" asked the Doctor softly. "What is the matter?"

"She is ill, very ill. I wonder, I am afraid she is going to die tonight." The words came in a frightened whisper.

It was as though he spoke of the present movement, in apprehension and fear, not of the past. The Big Business Man involuntarily rose in his chair, but the Doctor restrained him.

"She *is* ill? Now? What do you mean, Morton?"

The man's face showed a little confusion; he passed his hands over his eyes.

"Did I say that? It was so vivid. I forgot." He sighed, seemingly with relief. "Of course. I remember now. She did not die, I pulled her through. But it was a serious illness. Those long nights I sat at her bedside—my fear, and my love, my love for her!" He shook himself together. "I pulled her through, gentlemen. But it was a very terrible time."

The Very Young Man spoke up timidly. "Did you—did you live in Sumner long, Mr. Davis?"

Morton Davis inclined his head; then turned to smile at the Doctor as one who would understand him.

"It is not practical for a rising young physician to move about very much, is it, Frank? We lived there, let me see? Arthur was born in—in—"

"Your son?" asked the Big Business Man.

Again Morton Davis inclined his head gravely.

"Arthur was born in the fourth year our marriage. How time does fly when there is a child growing up around you, gentlemen. Those years of his infancy, his childhood, they seem to have passed so quickly, looking back on them now. I remember it was no time at all before he was eight years old—a snaggle-toothed, freckled-faced, tousled-haired little boy. And what a boy he was! The romps we had, those summer twilight evenings, in the garden there, back of the house!"

Morton Davis's face shone with the pride of fatherhood; his voice trembled with the recollections of the joy he had taken in his child, that little unborn son who only lived in the might have been.

THE PATHOS OF it must have struck the Big Business Man forcibly. He said something in a low tone aside to the Banker; the Banker answered gruffly. The Very Young Man sat hunched forward, hands clasped across his upraised knees. His face was flushed; his glistening eyes stared straight before him into vacancy.

"Your practice," said the Doctor, breaking another oppressive silence. "Were you very successful?"

"I was very successful, I suppose, yes," said Morton Davis. "After a few years, possibly the most successful physician in Sumner." He chuckled suddenly at some thought that came to him.

"I remember how coldly professional my manner was with my patients. You know, Frank. That reserve, that dignity. And yet Dora," he laughed outright, "Dora knew me for a young, impulsive, idealistic, romantic boy. That's what I was, really."

His voice became buoyant, enthusiastic. "Why, those

years Arthur was growing up! The romps I had with him. And then, after he had gone to bed, those quiet evenings I had with her. Our music. I used to think I was a great pianist in those days, and she did sing so beautifully! We used to go in to the opera in New York occasionally, not often, but enough so Dora learned many of them. And we had all the scores at home and studied them together.

"We were just like two young lovers all those years. I can remember how we used to go canoeing in the moonlight on the Sumner lake, she at my feet on a pile of cushions, singing softly out over the water; and my strokes in the rhythm of her song. Just like a young couple engaged; not as though we had a sturdy little boy lying asleep at home." His voice grew tender; he turned slightly toward the Doctor as though speaking to him alone, and ended.

"Those were wonderful, beautiful years to me, Frank, very, very beautiful years, indeed."

There followed another long silence. Morton Davis slouched lower in his chair, seeming to drift off again on the tide of his recollections.

After a time, the Banker rose noiselessly to his feet. His face betrayed unusual agitation. He bent over the Doctor and whispered tensely,

"All this he is thinking of is in the past, years ago. But the later years, last year, the *now?* My God man, how can it all end?"

The Very Young Man leaned over to them and whispered excitedly.

"Look at him now, Dr. Adams. Look. What is it?"

THE FIGURE OF Morton Davis still lay huddled in its chair. But every line of it was tense, rigid. On his face was an expression or horror, of tragedy, and a sorrow almost beyond endurance. The color had left his cheeks. The tears of an unnerved manhood welled in his eyes; his lips were pressed together as though to hold back a cry of anguish.

The Doctor jumped to his feet.

"What is it, Morton? Tell us. What is it?"

The man's lips moved, but at first no words came. Then he lifted sorrowful eyes to the friend's face.

"I cannot stand it, Frank," he whispered. "The horror of it. I—" His voice trailed away into silence. The other four men were all on their feet now, crowding toward him in sudden alarm.

"I—I cannot stand it," he repeated. "Both killed, Dora and—and my little boy; drowned out there on the lake yesterday. And now I am left alone, alone to face—"

The Big Business Man whispered to the Doctor.

"Bring him back, Frank. Quick. Say something. He is suffering too much. You—"

The Doctor laid his hand on Morton Davis's shoulder, shaking him a little.

"It's all right, Morton. Don't think of it any more. Look at me." He shook him more roughly. "Look at me, here. Don't you remember, here in the Scientific Club?"

The man in the chair started; his hands went to his eyes, like one awakening reluctantly from sleep. He sat up. The Doctor stepped back with a sigh of relief.

"I—of course, I remember. I'm all right now." Morton Davis smiled at the anxious men surrounding him. "It—I suppose the effect has worn off. The experiment is over, gentlemen. Has it taken long?"

The Doctor signed the other men to re-seat themselves.

"The experiment *is* over gentlemen," he said. "He has quite recovered, as you see. Perhaps, perhaps it would be better for us not to discuss it further this evening."

Morton Davis lighted another cigarette which the Very Young Man handed him. He seemed to have regained his composure, although he was still pale and appeared exhausted as though the strain had been too much for his strength.

"But I think—I think I should prefer to discuss it, gentlemen, a little," he said. "I can remember now quite clearly all I have said to you since I took that powder. I do not think I quite forgot where I was at all—except there just at the last."

He smiled wanly.

"So I would have lost her in a few years after all. And a little son, too. A curious thing, this might have been, gentlemen—these other roads to our life. Perhaps, what has been was for the best, for her, at any rate. I am glad, I think, that we did what we have done tonight. I know now what might have been. There is nothing hidden. What is to be, after she and I have died in this life, for that I am content to wait. I—"

THE BELL OF the telephone extension in the little private clubroom rang sharply. The Very Young Man rose to answer it.

"Mr. Davis? Yes, he's here. Just a moment." The Very Young Man turned in surprise, his hand over the mouthpiece of the instrument. "It's for you, Mr. Davis."

Morton Davis went to the telephone.

"I left word at my club I should be here," he said in explanation as he crossed the room.

"Mr. Davis? Yes, this is Morton Davis speaking. I—oh, thank you very much." He replaced the telephone receiver heavily and turned back to the center of the room. He took a few steps forward, then stopped, his figure swaying slightly. The color had entirely drained from his face, leaving it livid. He pulled himself together with a visible effort and continued on to his chair.

"It was my club, gentlemen," he said after a moment. "A telephone message came there a few moments ago; they forwarded it here to me. It said—it was from her husband. She—she died this evening, gentlemen. Just a little while ago, up there in her home on Riverside. "Very suddenly—pneumonia, they said. Her last request was that I be notified at once."

In the strained silence that followed one of the men murmured some words of sympathy. The others sat mute, with that gentle, helpless look that comes to a man whose feelings are too deeply touched for words.

Morton Davis strove to maintain his composure. His glance roved about the room a little wildly, coming finally to rest on the little vial, still partially filled with white powder, that the Doctor had left on the table. The lines about his mouth set grimly.

"Gentlemen, I—I wish to make a further experiment," he announced suddenly. "I'm going to take that powder again." He raised his hand toward the Doctor as though to stop objection.

"Not tonight, Morton," the Doctor protested. "You're overwrought."

"Tonight, now, it must be." There seemed an air of grim

determination about the man, and a little of irrationality, that would brook no interference.

He rose swiftly, dissolved the powder, drank it and reseated himself all in a moment. The four men watched him silently. He sat hunched low down in his chair, relaxed, his eyes wide open.

THE MINUTES PASSED and no one spoke. The hum of the street below became plainly audible in the silent room. For a long time, Morton Davis sat quiet, his eyes hardly blinking with the intensity of their stare. Slowly, his bloodless lips parted in a smile, then began to move.

"It is all so wonderful, so beautiful, here with her." Even in the heavy silence of the room the listening men could hardly catch the low-whispered words. "The soul—free at last—free."

The Doctor, meeting the Banker's apprehensive glance, half started from his chair.

"Free at last, free to be together." A look of ineffable happiness transfigured Morton Davis's face for an instant; his filming eyes widened.

"Free at last. I do not want to come back, I shall not come back. I—shall—not—" The murmured words trailed away.

The figure in the chair under the light suddenly stiffened, then related inert. The Very Young Man gave a low exclamation of fright. The Doctor leaped forward and bent over his friend. The Big Business Man hurriedly switched on the side globes, flooding the room with light.

After a moment, the Doctor straightened and looked sadly around him at the strained faces.

"He's dead, gentlemen," he said quietly.

THE PEPPERMINT TEST

1

"MR. QUIGLEY HIMSELF will be here any moment," said the Doctor. "I will give you the facts as briefly as I can."

"I know old man Quigley," the Chemist interjected. "He's been a member of the Scientific Club as long as any of us here. Most of us know him."

He appealed to the little group of men gathered in the private clubroom.

A chorus of nods answered him.

"Quite right," the Doctor agreed. "Mr. Quigley is also one of my patients—almost the only one I have retained since I gave up my medical practice for surgery. He came to my office yesterday on a personal matter that very narrowly escaped becoming a tragedy. It presents rather an interesting criminal problem. That is why I asked you gentlemen to come here tonight. The affair properly belongs with the police, of course; but I thought—and Mr. Quigley agrees with me—that if we could solve it here this evening before notifying the police—that would be the better way."

"What is the problem, Frank?" the Banker asked. "A tragedy, you said?"

"An averted tragedy. Here is the whole thing, gentlemen. As most of you know, Robert Quigley is a retired financier—a man now well in his eighties. He came to me yesterday in great perturbation, and announced that some of his family were trying to poison him."

"Good Lord!" exclaimed the Chemist. "Has he gone crazy?"

"I asked him that," said the Doctor. "But he was quite serious, and—well, facts are facts, no matter how amazing they may seem. I must tell you first that Mr. Quigley, for a year past, has had the obsession—I can hardly call it anything else—that his health demands the constant administration of small but very strong peppermint tablets at frequent intervals between meals."

The Doctor smiled slightly. "I have had to humor him on that—Heaven knows, peppermint is an innocent enough vice." His smile broadened as he met the eye of a brother physician. He added: "Perhaps they even do him good, for all I know—the human stomach is a most peculiar organ. At all events, Mr. Quigley is addicted to them. He takes eight or ten a day, I suppose—I've limited him to ten. Here is a bottle of them he purchased day before yesterday, and which yesterday morning he brought with him to my office." The Doctor produced a fairly large bottle of small white tablets.

"They are a foreign make," he continued. "Mr. Quigley likes them because they are so strong of peppermint flavor he considers them medicinal rather than a confection. He always buys the largest size bottle." The Doctor inspected the label. "Five hundred tablets it is supposed to contain."

"Did Quigley get poisoned from peppermint?" the Banker demanded. "What's the idea?"

The Doctor laid the bottle on the table, under an electrolier. He said solemnly: "Gentlemen, I have found by analyzation that each of these innocuous-looking little tablets contains one and one-half grains of strychnine—a fatal dose under most conditions!"

"Good heavens!" the Astronomer exclaimed. "Enough in that bottle to kill five hundred people!"

There was a chorus of similar ejaculations.

The Big Business Man asked: "How did Quigley ever discover anything was wrong with them? I should think the first one he took would have—"

"Nothing saved him but the utmost good luck," the Doctor rejoined. "Gentlemen, at the age of eighty odd Mr. Quigley is an extraordinarily methodical man. He always does things the same way—and that fact saved his life yesterday. Peppermint tablets, as you doubtless know, are not usually swallowed intact; generally they are allowed to dissolve in the mouth. Mr. Quigley, however, has his own method, from which he never departs. He nibbles at them—holds them in his hand and bites off tiny fragments, as though they were a dainty morsel of candy—which, indeed, I believe he really considers them, for all his swearing by their medicinal efficacy. Thus he found the taste of these bitter and unpleasant."

"I don't see why he should blame the poisoning on his family," remarked the Playwright. "Where did he get that bottle of peppermints?"

"The circumstances of the case are simple and fairly conclusive," said the Doctor. "Mr. Quigley personally bought that bottle—"

The Alienist interjected: "Let us assume there was no strychnine in them when they were purchased."

"I think so," agreed the Doctor. "We can eliminate

the possibility of any poison being injected into them in the drug store. There is no motive. Mr. Quigley is totally unknown to this particular store. He just happened to be passing in his car, and stopped off and bought this bottle at random from the counter. His usual place was out of them, and he had some difficulty in locating another that carried this particular foreign brand."

"When did he buy them, did you say?" the Banker asked.

"Night before last. There is additional proof that the substitution of these poison tablets for the original peppermints was made in Mr. Quigley's home. The evening he bought them he took one, without unusual result. He left them, during that night, in the medicine cabinet of his bathroom. After breakfast the next morning—yesterday— he took a second tablet, with the result I have described. Then he brought them to me."

"In other words," summarized the Lawyer, "it is obvious that during that night, or breakfast time yesterday, someone of his household substituted the poison."

The Doctor nodded. "That certainly seems a reasonable assumption. It is rather far-fetched to suppose that someone from outside would break in for that purpose."

"What do *you* propose to do, Doctor?" asked the Very Young Man diffidently.

The Author interjected: "Somebody in Mr. Quigley's family is trying to murder him; with what motive?"

"For his money," the Banker retorted, "He's worth four millions. Isn't that motive enough?"

The Doctor went on quietly: "I am assuming for his money—therefore I eliminate all members of his household except those mentioned substantially in his will. He has gone over the document with me, and he tells me also that his family are familiar with its main points."

"That strengthens the motive," commented the Lawyer.

The Chemist started a question, but the Doctor waved him aside. "Just a moment. If you gentlemen will allow me these assumptions as facts, then we reach this one conclusion: some one or more of four specific people must have tried deliberately to murder Mr. Quigley. Should this conclusion prove to be correct, I propose to determine here in this room tonight who is guilty and who innocent. To that end I have invited them all to come here with Mr. Quigley—they should arrive at any moment. I used an entirely extraneous pretext, of course; but I want you gentlemen to know in advance that I am going to put them to a test which I hope—and believe—may show us plainly which of them is guilty."

"Mr. Quigley said nothing of the affair at home?" asked the Big Business Man.

"Not a word. He came to me at once. I have told him to act as though nothing unusual had happened. I don't want suspicion aroused. If the police were to go after this—with 'bull-in-a-china-shop' methods—I doubt if the solution would ever be reached. I have told Mr. Quigley what I propose doing this evening. Beyond that, nothing has been said or done."

"What *do* you propose doing, Doctor?" asked the Very Young Man again.

"Who are these people coming?" the Astronomer demanded. "You said there were four?"

"Mr. Quigley himself and four others: Mr. and Mrs. James Robins—they are Mr. Quigley's married daughter and her husband; Charles R. Quigley, his brother; and Mrs. Billings, Mr. Quigley's housekeeper—a widow who has been in the family some twenty years. There are several other servants, but none of them are mentioned in the will except by very small legacies."

"Have we reason to suspect anyone particularly?" the Lawyer asked. "What does Quigley think? Is there any ill feeling in the family?"

"He secretly dislikes his son-in-law intensely," the Doctor answered. "An old man's whim, I should say. I have always found James Robins rather a decent little chap. Charles Quigley, personally, I don't happen to like. He's never been in business—lives on the moderate inheritance which he and his brother had from their father. I don't believe it was much. Robert Quigley is a self-made man. Charles is a bachelor—a man now about fifty. He's abroad much of the time—rather a sportsman, I understand; goes on hunting expeditions and the like."

"He sounds promising," commented the Playwright. "Robert got rich in business; Charles stayed poor going on hunting expeditions."

"Tell us about Mrs. Billings, the housekeeper," the Author suggested. "Is she the kind who would commit murder?"

The Doctor smiled. "No, I should not say so. Nor any of them, for that matter. I should not like to accuse any one of them of such a crime, and I have no intention of doing so. That, in a way, is what makes the affair interesting. The guilty person must be trapped without an accusation."

The Playwright reverted to his original idea. "Tell us more about the brother. What does Quigley himself think?"

"I don't know—I wouldn't discuss it with him," the Doctor declared. "Gentlemen, I think all this sort of thing is futile. We could go on theorizing about these people indefinitely, and then, probably, we would overlook the one vital point that might show us the solution. The police might proceed after that fashion. What are the relative amounts to be inherited? The character of the people? Their need of additional immediate money? Which one could most easily have obtained the drug and prepared the tablets? Whence were they obtained? Prove that some particular one of them *did* purchase strychnine—and you have the criminal!

"These are police methods. But, gentlemen, we are not trained to that. Let us ignore all theory. For my part, if one of these four is guilty, all I want is to have them in this room. I will accuse no one. I will not mention this intended crime—in fact, I will keep as far from it as I can. But the murderer, if he is one of them, will show himself to us. Of that I am convinced."

"But, Doctor," protested the Chemist, "there are so many things—"

He stopped abruptly as the door opened and an attendant announced:

"Mr. Robert Quigley and family would like to see Dr. Adams."

"Bring them up," ordered the Doctor.

The door closed. The Doctor put the bottle of peppermint tablets back into his pocket and added hastily: "Say very little, gentlemen. Show no surprise at anything I may say or do. If I suggest anything, agree to it. Do what I tell you."

The men settled
themselves casually
about the room, and a
moment later their visi-
tors entered. Robert
Quigley, the man who
had so narrowly escaped
death, was rather an
energetic-looking octo-
genarian—a wizened,
frail body, smooth-
shaven, stern-featured
face deeply lined, and a
bald spot fringed with snow-white hair—but alert and
dogmatic in manner. His daughter was a sweet-faced,
gentle-looking woman of about thirty-five, fashionably
and expensively dressed. Her husband appeared to be
about the same age, his neat little brown mustache, pink
cheeks and mincingly courteous manner making him seem
distinctly effeminate.

Charles Quigley, the old man's brother, was a man about
fifty—tall, lean and muscular, iron-gray hair, smooth-
shaven face, and with an unmistakable outdoor look about
him. He carried himself with a complacent air, as though
conscious of a great personal superiority. He was dressed
in a rough tweed suit of English cut.

Mrs. Billings, in an unnaturally brown false-front, and
dressed at her best for the occasion, was a stoutish woman
of around fifty-five. Her demeanor was that of a privileged
family retainer.

Such were the members of the household of Robert

Quigley, octogenarian millionaire, from among whom, without accusing any one of them, the Doctor had determined to pick a potential murderer. The room was in confusion a moment, while greetings were exchanged and introductions made. All the visitors, with the exception of the octogenarian himself, obviously were surprised at the number of men gathered to meet them.

When they were comfortably seated the Doctor explained:

"As you know, ladies and gentlemen, Mr. Robert Quigley is a member of the Scientific Club here. The rest of us are also. We are engaged—largely for diversion—in the solution of such scientific problems as may arise among the club members.

"Occasionally one of us may evolve a scientific theory which he wishes to test. Or again, one of us may have made some scientific discovery which, before giving it to the world, he desires to discuss and perfect. For these reasons we frequently meet in one of these private clubrooms, just as we have tonight—with such visitors as may be necessary for our experiment."

He paused a moment, looking about impartially over the assembled group. Then he continued:

"The specific reason for our being here this evening is to demonstrate a discovery of my own, on which I have been working for some years. I spoke to Mr. Quigley about it two or three weeks ago, as a brother club member. He was much interested, and suggested that I give a private demonstration to a few other members, using you ladies and gentlemen of his own family as subjects."

Quite evidently, from the expressions on their faces, this

announcement was not altogether pleasing to the visitors. They looked at each other in surprise and apprehension. Charles Quigley remarked with some asperity:

"It strikes me you take a good deal for granted, Dr. Adams. Suppose we do not wish—"

"He takes nothing for granted," the octogenarian interrupted testily. "*I* volunteered your services. You'll do as I tell you—all of you."

"Glory be!" ejaculated Mrs. Billings.

The Doctor laughed good-naturedly.

"Naturally you ladies and gentlemen are apprehensive at being made the subjects of an experiment you know nothing about. I assure you there is nothing to fear—in fact, the whole thing is quite to your interest. Let me explain further. Mr. Quigley, in these latter years of his life, naturally wishes to plan the division of his estate with the utmost justice. I am going to speak quite frankly to you now—to Mr. Quigley himself as well.

"When a man reaches the age of eighty he becomes—well, peculiar—childish, even—in many ways." The Doctor glanced at the octogenarian and smiled quizzically. "You did not know I was going to expose you this way, did you, Mr. Quigley? But that is true, my friends. Mr. Quigley is peculiar, though he does not think so. He takes unreasonable likes and dislikes."

"If you will permit me to say so," interposed the cherubic-looking son-in-law, "I don't see what you're getting at, Dr. Adams."

"You will in a moment. I may tell you all I am more than Mr. Quigley's medical adviser. In fact, I am proud to say

I am rather his personal adviser as well—and one of his best friends."

The Doctor's glance at Charles Quigley was impishly malicious. He added: "Mr. Quigley confides everything to me. For instance, hardly a month ago he came to me, having about decided to disinherit his sister Jane in California because she had not written to him in several weeks."

The old man's daughter rose and seated herself on the arm of his chair, caressing his hair.

"Father dear," she said with soft reproof, "how could you be so silly?"

At the Doctor's bland smile when he paused Charles Quigley observed sourly: "You talk in circles, Dr. Adams. Just what is this experiment you want to make us take part in? How does it concern *us?*"

The Doctor's manner abruptly changed. He retorted sharply:

"It concerns all of you very vitally. Mr. Quigley is about to alter materially his will. He is going to discuss it here—tonight—in the presence of all these gentlemen."

The Doctor waited until the surprise of this statement had passed. Mr. Quigley's relatives exchanged startled glances; Mrs. Billings leaned forward in her chair, vague hope, anxiety and fear mingled in her expression.

The Doctor went on: "We are going to discuss frankly how Mr. Quigley should divide his estate. Rather an unusual proceeding? Yes, doubtless—but Mr. Quigley's whims are law in such a matter. More than that, I am going to call upon each of you to give your *honest* opinion as to what the terms of his new will shall be."

"You can leave me out," declared the financier's brother. "When a man gets so childish—"

Old man Quigley started to his feet in anger, but the Doctor waved him back.

"Just a moment! You—Mr. Charles Quigley—will do as you are told." There was no mistaking the authority in the Doctor's tone, or the fact that he *did* personally dislike the financier's brother.

The old man's daughter said mildly:

"But, Dr. Adams, don't you see we can't discuss such a matter. We cannot talk about—"

"Mrs. Robins," the Doctor interrupted courteously, "I realize quite well how awkward a thing it is. However, I assure you Mr. Quigley is determined it shall be done—so determined, in fact, that if any of you refuse you will be left out of the will almost entirely."

At this Mrs. Billings murmured: "I wouldn't never cross him." And the son-in-law said meekly: "We want to do as father wishes, of course."

"I believe that," answered the Doctor with apparent frankness. He exchanged a swift glance with the Alienist, whose expression seemed to indicate that he was wholly puzzled by the proceedings.

The Doctor went on quickly: "This affair is not so purposeless as it sounds, my friends. To ask prospective heirs what they think they should inherit is unusual and doubtless somewhat useless. But to ask them what they *honestly* think—and to have a means of making them honest—well, that should be interesting, at least."

The Doctor's keen glance seemed carefully measuring the effect of his words.

"Ladies and gentlemen," he continued quietly, "for over four years I have been experimenting with a chemical which would so influence the mind that—temporarily at least—complete frankness of speech would result. That was my goal. I have not reached it—but I have gone a considerable distance. You think I am not wholly serious? Why, that is hardly so revolutionary a thing as you perhaps consider it. Under the influence of alcohol, for instance, a man talks much more openly than otherwise. You all know that."

His darting glance held each of his listeners in turn. He added easily: "Mr. Quigley is interested because I have told him that I can, with a potable fluid I have prepared, make anyone tell me his honest, sincere convictions on any subject."

Charles Quigley laughed ironically.

"You're to be congratulated, Doctor," he observed. "How does it work?"

The Doctor did not smile. "A scientific explanation of why alcohol and many well-known drugs loosen the tongue would weary you, probably—nor would you understand it. My preparation goes a little further than that, however. I have been able—very temporarily, of course—to make the memory more vivid; to recall to the subject's mind many little details that seemingly have long since been forgotten. This is important, my friends.

"For instance, Mr. Quigley feels that many of you have been unjust to him in the past—have been unkind. You have forgotten these little incidents, but he has not—since they impressed his mind more than yours. He wants you to recall them, for if you are to tell him frankly what you consider you deserve from him at his death you must have all the facts at your command."

The Doctor stepped behind a screen and produced a five-gallon glass bottle, such as spring water is sold in. It was about half full of a clear fluid, with a very slight tinge of color. He set the bottle on the center table.

"I prepared this drink about two hours ago," he said. "Jack, will you go out and get that tray of glasses? Eight or ten full-size tumblers will do."

The Very Young Man hastened away.

The Doctor added: "You need not be afraid of this, my friends. I shall drink some with you, as well as Mr. Quigley himself, and one or two of the rest of us. It is quite harmless."

He added as an afterthought: "You will experience no unpleasant sensations—I give you my word on that. Nor is it intoxicating, so that you will be tempted to talk of things you do not wish to mention. As a matter of fact, you will hardly know you have had more than a drink of water, which, indeed, is its principal ingredient."

"And anyone who don't want to drink it with me," declared Mr. Quigley grimly, "needn't expect any of *my* money. I'm sick of asking favors of people who don't care anything about me."

The Very Young Man returned with a tray of tumblers, and he and the Doctor filled them from the huge bottle.

The Doctor raised a glass. "Come, gentlemen, who will be the first to drink?"

No one answered.

"Very well," said the Doctor. "I will start."

He drained the tumbler. "Who next?" he asked.

"I will," volunteered the Very Young Man.

He drained his glass also, bravado making him swallow it down without preliminary tasting.

The Doctor offered a third glass to the octogenarian, who drank its contents without hesitation.

"Pass around the tray, Jack," said the Doctor.

The Alienist took a glass, and one or two of the other men. Mrs. Billings drank hers with obvious apprehension, meanwhile trying to smile ingratiatingly at her master. Charles Quigley was contemptuous, draining his glass with a sneer. The financier's daughter and her husband were both rather solemn, but after a moment of hesitation followed the rest.

The Very Young Man collected the empty glasses.

"There," said the Doctor. "That was not so very formidable, was it? My chemicals normally have rather a disagreeable taste, but in deference to you I masked it, at the last moment, with peppermint—though you notice even the mint flavor is hardly perceptible. I used Mr. Quigley's fresh bottle of peppermint tablets when he was here this afternoon—we didn't have a thing here that would do."

He spoke rapidly and quite casually, producing simultaneously the peppermint bottle—only this time it was empty, for he had removed its cork and spilled the contents into his pocket.

He added ironically: "Mr. Quigley's peppermint tablets make good flavoring, my friends."

The Doctor waited, tense and with eyes narrowed, for the effect of his words. To the financier's relatives, obviously, they held nothing alarming; but Mrs. Billings's face had slowly drained of its blood. She stared at the peppermint bottle as though hypnotized; and then, with a low moan, crumpled and fell unconscious to the floor. The Doctor sprang to his feet.

"Dr. Gregg, will you lift her up? The couch there. Jack, you help him. She has fainted."

He turned to the others, who were in confusion.

"Do not be alarmed, my friends. What we drank was merely water—flavored with a little mint and vanilla."

They carried the inert form of the housekeeper to the couch, while the Doctor briefly explained the circumstances to Mr. Quigley's amazed family.

A few moments later the Alienist, from his chair by the couch, said quietly:

"She is all right now. She has confessed. Her son—in Philadelphia—made her do it, for her fifteen-thousand-dollar legacy."

"By the almighty, I never thought of him!" old man Quigley exclaimed excitedly. "He works in a drug store. He—"

The Doctor interrupted, addressing the club members: "You see, gentlemen? That is a police detail—we did not need it. Jack, will you telephone police headquarters?" He added quietly: "I think that is all, my friends. I am glad to have exonerated you."

A DARK-ROOM CONVICTION

1

"IT MOST CERTAINLY is a case of arson, gentlemen," said the Doctor earnestly. His eyes swept the interested little group of men in the clubroom and rested on the face of an alert-looking young man beside him. "Mr. James Martin, here, is adjuster for the Globe Protective Association. He has been given this claim to adjust. It is important to him—it means a promotion if he can avoid the payment of this seventeen thousand dollars. That is why I propose this experiment, here tonight. Mr. Martin and his wife are very good friends of mine."

The Banker regarded the youthful visitor with renewed interest. "That's a lot of money, young man." He added to the Doctor: "You say you're morally sure it's arson, and no one can ever prove it? How is that, Frank?"

The Doctor nodded. "Here are the circumstances, gentlemen. The Globe Protective Association wrote a policy covering the factory stock of an individual in Rosewood, New Jersey—one Arthur Jackson."

The Lawyer smiled. "I judge he had a fire."

"He did. His factory—a ramshackle, one-story building—burned to the ground about eleven in the evening, just a week ago. Jackson's business, gentlemen, was the buying of old clothes in quantity. He stored them in this building, where several girls mended and pressed them.

The product was then sold to small, ready-made clothiers; of the type advertising 'tailors' misfits.' "

Several of the men nodded. The Doctor went on:

"Jackson owns the land on which the factory stood. He also owned the building, which was uninsured. The stock was totally destroyed, and upon that he is about to collect seventeen thousand dollars—unless we can prevent it. I've asked him to come here this evening. He'll be here presently."

"Where was Jackson at the time of the fire?" the Chemist asked.

"He was at home, about two blocks away. More than that, he had been at home for the whole evening. He was playing cards with friends." The Doctor's smile was lugubrious. "His alibi is perfect."

"Doesn't sound much like arson," commented the Banker.

"Mr. Martin's suspicions were first aroused," the Doctor resumed quietly, "by the fact that, only two days before the fire, Jackson had a handsome offer for the purchase of his land—without the building. It was falling down, anyway; a suburban apartment house is to be erected in its stead."

"What motive—" the Astronomer began.

"The motive, gentlemen, is there, I'm sure. Jackson's stock—old clothes, you understand—was doubtless overvalued. His fixtures and machinery—a few pressing-machines—amount to almost nothing. By this method he disposes of his stock, all at once and for cash, without the trouble of moving it somewhere else and selling it piece-meal. He has already accepted the offer for his land."

"What is the evidence for arson?" demanded the Lawyer.

"Very little, perhaps, from a legal standpoint. Mr. Martin learned from neighbors that the factory was totally dark at ten forty-five p.m., and five minutes later it was a mass of flames inside. That in itself is curious. Leaking gas from within the factory was noticeable in the neighborhood for an hour before the fire. And, to fit my own theory of how Jackson might have started it and still have been at home playing cards all the evening, Mr. Martin found in the ruins a very extraordinary piece of one-inch, iron pipe, nearly ten feet long—extraordinary because it was perforated all over with tiny holes like a sieve!"

There was a moment of silence. "Does Jackson know you are after him?" the Big Business Man asked.

The Doctor shook his head. "Mr. Martin told him nothing of these discoveries. But he did tentatively suggest arson, and the man laughed. He says you couldn't prove anything against him, and in that he probably is quite correct. I myself have no intention of accusing him—that is, not directly—and certainly not in court."

"What is your theory of how he did it, Doctor Adams?" the Very Young Man asked timidly.

Before the Doctor could answer, an attendant entered.

"Mr. Arthur Jackson to see Doctor Adams."

"Show him up at once," ordered the Doctor. He rose to his feet.

"I'm sorry I won't have time to explain further," he added briskly. "I've gone to considerable preparation here tonight. But all you need to know, gentlemen, is that I have arranged a scientific experiment—a test, if you like—and that, if this Jackson is guilty of arson, I believe he will show us so plainly."

The Banker protested. "But what do we—"

"Just follow my lead, gentlemen. You'll soon see what I'm after."

The door opened, and Arthur Jackson stood on the threshold. He was a small, gray-haired man of about sixty, dressed in ordinary business clothes, with a huge gold watch chain and pendant fob crossing his vest, and a very large diamond stud in his shirt front, as predominating features. In a business situation, Mr. Jackson would undoubtedly have maintained complete self-possession. As he entered this room of the Scientific Club, however—with nearly a score of keen-eyed, professional men all staring at him curiously—he was obviously not his usual suave self. He stood in the doorway, surprised by this unexpected gathering, and gazing around almost stupidly.

The Doctor had seated himself among the others. He now stood up. "Come in, Mr. Jackson. I am Doctor Adams."

Jackson advanced, and they shook hands. The Doctor's cordial greeting seemed to put the visitor more at his ease. His glance lighted on Jimmy Martin, and he nodded affably.

The Doctor pushed forward an easy-chair. "Sit down, Mr. Jackson. These gentlemen are all my friends and fellow members of the club—Mr. Martin you know."

Jackson nodded again, smiling impartially at the men in acknowledgment of this introduction. Casting his hat on the table, he seated himself comfortably. He crossed his legs and produced a cigar.

"Can I smoke in here?" he asked.

The Very Young Man, taking his cue from the Doctor,

solicitously lighted a match and held it. Jackson beamed his thanks. His manner was perfectly self-assured now.

"Much obliged, young man. Now, Doctor Adams, could you tell me what your business is with me? I got your letter—"

"I will," agreed the Doctor. "You must allow me to explain it to these gentlemen at the same time. They are as interested in science as I am." He pushed his chair backward, to bring all the men in front of him.

"Gentlemen," he began, "Mr. Jackson has come here tonight as a great kindness to me, to act as the subject of a scientific demonstration which I wish to lay before you."

The Doctor paused. Jackson nodded genially. Quite evidently, he enjoyed being the center of the conversation, even though he had only a vague idea of what it was about. The Doctor continued:

"I may say, also, that this experiment, should it prove successful, will benefit Mr. Jackson as well."

This the visitor could understand readily. It was, to be exact, the specific reason why he had come. His nod was more emphatic than before. The Doctor resumed:

"I will tell you very briefly, gentlemen, that Mr. Jackson is faced with a most annoying situation. He recently had an entirely unexpected offer to sell a piece of property without the building standing upon it—a small factory. Almost simultaneously, this factory, which was uninsured, burned down. Mr. Jackson was at home that evening, playing cards. This fact is proven—it cannot be disputed. And yet, because of the coincidence of these two events, the insurance company who wrote a policy on the burned stock now seems trying to prove that in some miraculous way Mr. Jackson committed arson."

Certainly, the Doctor had presented the visitor's case very clearly. Jackson beamed.

The Chemist spoke up. "You weren't near your factory at the time of the fire, Mr. Jackson?"

"I was not," declared the visitor in disgust. "You couldn't make sense out of it at all. This here young man"—his glance to Jimmy Martin was wholly without animosity—"y'understan' I ain't blamin' him. When a man's in business—"

"He must be zealous in his employer's interests," the Doctor finished with a smile. "But, gentlemen, Mr. Martin, here, is a little too zealous. He will get his company into trouble—that's what I fear."

"What is your experiment, Frank?" the Banker demanded.

The Doctor continued blandly: "On the other hand, gentlemen, this insurance company undoubtedly could cause Mr. Jackson considerable annoyance. Even now, I believe, they threaten to make him sue them for his money. If they do that, however, as I told Mr. Martin, I think he would beat them in the end."

"An' if they keep on talkin' about this arson business, I could get ten thousand dollars damages extra," the visitor asserted.

"Possibly," the Doctor agreed. "But you don't want that kind of action. Nor does Mr. Martin's company. Therefore, gentlemen, I propose to secure proof that may perhaps enable Mr. Jackson to collect his seventeen thousand dollars without additional delay. That is why he came here."

Jackson seemed to understand all this perfectly. He uncrossed his legs, spreading his large feet luxuriously over the rug, his cigar in one hand, the other toying idly with his huge watch chain.

"And if I could help you with this science business, Doctor Adams," he declared largely, "I would consider it a great pleasure."

"Thank you," and the Doctor nodded. He continued to address the room in general. "Gentlemen, I know you are all eager to hear specifically of the experiment I am about to make. You are no more eager for it than I am, for it will be my first semi-public demonstration of a theory on which I have been working for some years." He smiled slightly. "That is to say, I have been theorizing, and Mr. Jensen, here"—his nod indicated a blond, athletic-looking man of thirty-odd—"has done all the real work. It is due to his efforts entirely that we are enabled to perform the experiment."

The Lawyer, sitting beside Jackson, whispered: "What's he getting at? Do you know?"

"I couldn't give you the least idea," responded the visitor.

The Doctor continued: "My theory, gentlemen, concerns the scientific aspect of thought. For an analogous case, let us take music. Music is, scientifically speaking, merely a matter of vibration. The timbre of a violin differs from the timbre of a piano only in the variety of its wavelengths. One note differs from another only in the rate of vibration."

"You mean that thought has something to do with vibration?" the Playwright asked.

"Thought is vibration," the Doctor answered quietly. "In its physical sense, it is exactly that—inaudible vibration."

This discussion was obviously far over Jackson's head. He was still smiling complacently, evidently clinging to the Doctor's last intelligible statement, a proof that his innocence of this ridiculous arson charge was soon to be forthcoming.

The Doctor was proceeding earnestly: "Vibration is one of the most fundamental attributes of matter. Sound, light, heat, the telephone, wireless, the X-ray—all are vibration in different forms."

"How can you prove thought is vibration?" the Big Business Man asked.

"It has been proven many times," declared the Doctor. "I am going to prove it tonight—in a few moments. But do not think I originated the idea. The pioneers in this field agree that thought is merely waves of vibration, starting from nerve centers of the brain—waves of smaller magnitude and greater frequency than those which constitute the X-ray."

"That would explain thought transference very simply, wouldn't it?" the Astronomer said, half to himself, "with another brain as a sort of receiving station for the vibrations."

"Exactly," agreed the Doctor. "It is the most rational explanation I have ever heard advanced."

"Assuming it to be so, in what way have you applied it?" the Lawyer asked.

"To the art of photography," the Doctor answered readily. "The basis of photography is the action of light vibrations upon silver salts. The X-ray has been adapted to photography. And we are not without evidence that photographic plates are sensitive to other vibrations as well—vibrations which in themselves are totally unknown to science."

"Meaning what?" demanded the Banker.

"I mean spirit photographs, George. You've seen some, haven't you?"

The Banker nodded.

"I do not mean to liken thought photography to spirit photography," the Doctor added quickly. "The photographing of thoughts is infinitely more understandable. It is merely a question of preparing an emulsion sensitive to these thought vibrations which are of very small magnitude and very great frequency. That Mr. Jensen has accomplished, gentlemen, and we are now prepared to photograph Mr. Jackson's thoughts, to the end that we may prove him innocent even of the thought of crime."

This calm statement caused a stir in the room. The Doctor was watching Jackson narrowly. The visitor was obviously startled—as well he might have been, whether innocent or guilty.

"I—I don't want to be—" he stammered; but the Doctor interrupted suavely:

"Do not be alarmed, my friend. Naturally, to one not of scientific mind, such an idea is disturbing. I assure you there is no danger—no more than in having any photographer make your portrait."

Jackson's poise seemed thoroughly shaken. He stared toward the door, sitting bolt upright and gripping the arms of his chair, like a dentist's patient suddenly confronted with a wicked-looking pair of forceps.

The Doctor laughed at him. "I tell you there is no physical danger. If you were a criminal now, you would give immediate proof of your guilt by refusing the experiment." The Doctor raised his hand deprecatingly. "All you need do is concentrate your mind firmly upon that card game you were playing at home that evening—and we will attempt to photograph your thoughts. We may not succeed, of course; but, in any event, I give you my word you will not experience even the slightest physical discomfort."

Something the Doctor said must have partially allayed Jackson's fears, for he relaxed, mopping the perspiration from his forehead with a huge silk handkerchief.

The Lawyer murmured, half to himself: "These scientists kid themselves a lot. I don't believe there's anything in this at all."

The visitor turned and nodded a grateful agreement. "Me, too. You can't make sense out of it." He drew a deep breath. "You can count on me, Doctor Adams," he declared magnanimously.

"Thank you," acknowledged the Doctor quietly. "Jack, help me with this table, will you?"

The Very Young Man sprang to his feet, and they moved the center table over against the wall. Most of the men shifted their chairs, clearing the center of the room. Jackson, with panic again growing in his eyes, stood up uncertainly, and someone whisked his chair away.

The Photographer meanwhile had folded back a huge screen that had closed off nearly a third of the room. A battery of six small cameras, standing on tripods, was revealed. Around them stood several light screens and reflectors—black and white cloth stretched on circular metal frames, with roller bases and adjustments for tilting at various angles.

Jackson stared at all this in alarm. The Photographer bustled into a little improvised dark-room that stood in a corner of the chamber. In a moment he was out again. "All ready, Doctor Adams."

The Doctor advanced with a small, cane-seated chair. "If you please, Mr. Jackson. Where shall I seat him, Mr. Jenson? Sit down, gentlemen—out of the way, all of you."

The Photographer seated Jackson in the center of the room, facing the six cameras. The subject of the experiment smiled a somewhat sickly smile; his eye met the Lawyer's, and the Lawyer winked at him; reassuringly.

"What next, Mr. Jensen?" The Doctor stood regarding the scene, and then seated himself out of the way. "Jack, help Mr. Jensen."

Assisted by the Very Young Man, the Photographer placed two black screens behind Jackson for a background, and two white ones at his left. At his right, some six feet away, was placed a flashlight pan, standing on a pedestal. Jackson eyed it fearfully.

"Quite all right, Mr. Jackson," the Doctor reassured him. "Merely a little puff of flash-light powder. I may mention, gentlemen, that a very important part of Mr. Jensen's task was the preparation of this powder. Ordinary flash light is very white—a pure actinic light. Ours, however, is very different. It makes rather a poor portrait, but on our special plate emulsion it records thought vibrations—which is the only thing we are after."

When the cameras had been focused and the plate holders placed in them, with the slides removed, the Photographer produced two small glass bottles. He eyed them carefully against the light, shook them, and removed the corks. Into the pan he poured a small quantity of powder from each—estimated it—added a little more. Then he said:

"We want almost no light, Doctor Adams. Then I can open the shutters."

The Doctor switched off the lights, leaving only one dim bulb lighted in the table electrolier. Huge shadows sprang up about the room; a fantastic black shape of Jackson spread itself grotesquely across the floor and up the opposite wall. In the breathless silence only the Photographer's agile footsteps were audible. The clicks of the camera shutters, as he opened them one by one, sounded startlingly loud.

"What is it I do, Doctor Adams?" Jackson's voice was strained, terrified. "You could tell me what it is I must think about—"

The Photographer struck a match and lighted a little wax taper. Jackson shifted his position in fright. The Doctor's voice, suddenly stern, said:

"You must forget you are here. Think carefully just what you were doing the night of the fire. You dismissed your employees at closing time. You—went over your books, alone in the factory. Or did you? You know what you did! Whatever it was, think of it now—detail by detail."

The Doctor was still talking when the Photographer applied his lighted taper to the powder. There came a brief puff of dazzlingly white light, followed by a slower-burning, peculiar, reddish glare, which lasted several seconds.

Jackson, after one involuntary start, sat like a stone image. The Photographer hastened to his cameras, closing their shutters.

"All over, Doctor Adams. Lights, please."

The lights flashed on. Jackson shook himself and tried to smile, evidently pleased that he was still alive. The Doctor stood up; the room was in commotion from the whispered comments of the onlookers and the movement of their chairs.

"There, Mr. Jackson, that was not so very formidable, was it? Take a more comfortable chair. Jack, get someone to help you put the table back. And open a window and let that smoke out."

The Photographer, plate holders in hand, was starting for the little dark-room. "Five minutes for developing, Doctor Adams."

The Doctor sat beside Jackson, and the Lawyer joined them. Several of the other men moved nearer, addressing the visitor. Jackson gradually recovered his poise.

"I hope you made this experiment a success, Doctor Adams," he declared pleasantly. "I ain't much on this science business. Maybe you can shut up this insurance company now so I get my seventeen thousand dollars."

The Doctor nodded. "But we may have failed. It is not always possible to—"

The Photographer abruptly called from within the dark-room:

"Oh, Mr. Adams—will you step here a moment?"

The tense note of excitement in his voice was unmistakable. The Doctor looked around in surprise, exchanging glances with several of his friends.

The Photographer called more insistently: "Doctor Adams—come here, please."

Jackson sensed the expectancy of those around him.

Anxiety came into his face. "What is it he wants, Doctor Adams?"

"All right, Jensen, I'm coming." The Doctor sprang up and hastened into the little enclosure.

The men all sat silent. From within the tiny dark-room, where an electric fan was now buzzing, came the indistinguishable whispers of the two men. The Photographer was evidently greatly excited. Suddenly his voice broke above a whisper.

"I tell you he's committed arson, Doctor! Look! You can't miss it! Here—look at this one—a long iron pipe on the floor with a lot of holes in it!"

"Talk lower! Wait!" came the Doctor's admonition.

"No! Look here. See, here's where he's connecting it up with a gas outlet!" The Photographer's excitement rose beyond control. "Oh, Jack! Jack Bruce. Lock the doors— don't let him out! Phone for the police!"

It took several seconds for the meaning of this sudden outburst to sink into Jackson's intelligence. When it did, he sprang to his feet, his face ashen. "That's a lie! You couldn't prove it. I was thinking of something else! What is this science—"

The Very Young Man, his eyes blazing, confronted him. "You sit down, you. Don't you dare move till Doctor Adams comes out."

The Lawyer reached for the telephone, holding it in his lap.

Jackson sat down. From the dark-room came the Doctor, more excited than most of his friends had ever seen him. The Photographer was close behind, three or four small, dripping plates in his hands.

"A most extraordinary thing, gentlemen!" the Doctor exclaimed. "Astounding! I never would have—" He stopped abruptly, facing Jackson. "I am forced to the unpleasant necessity of handing you over to the police," he added coldly. "Will someone please get police headquarters on the wire? I'll talk to them."

The Lawyer obediently raised the receiver.

"Wait!" ejaculated the now thoroughly terrified Jackson. "Wait! You can't do that! Tell me what them pictures show. You can't prove nothing. I—"

"Oh, can't we?" the Photographer demanded. "How about—"

The Doctor cut in vehemently: "Tell it in court, Jensen— not now. The pictures speak for themselves."

Jimmy Martin, who throughout the entire proceedings had sat dumbly watching in awe, now exploded: "I knew he was a crook!"

And the Photographer added: "You said it, Martin!" He waved his wet glass rectangles. "Take a look, anybody. A piece of iron pipe, ten feet long or so, perforated with holes, connected to the gas. He turned on the gas and covered up the pipe with a lot of rubbish. A fuse or something sets it off a few hours later! A puff—the whole inside of the building is in flames with some of the windows blown out! Take a look. It's all here!"

No one could have read from Jackson's expression anything but that this was all fairly close to the truth. The Photographer held one of his negatives in front of Jackson's face, between his eyes and the light. What Jackson saw was his own figure sitting in the chair a few moments before. And in the air above his head was a fairly clear reproduction of a piece of iron pipe, perforated with a myriad of tiny holes. Jackson shuddered and looked away. The Photographer laughed sarcastically and retreated in triumph to his dark-room, carrying the negatives with him.

The Lawyer was now speaking softly into the telephone. Jackson came back to himself abruptly. "Wait!" he exclaimed again. "Let's talk this thing over. Ain't that more businesslike? You couldn't do business in a hurry like this. Everybody gets excited right off the bat." He mopped his brow vigorously.

The Lawyer hung up the receiver. Jimmy Martin came forward at the Doctor's glance. "I have my company's offer of settlement here, if you'd like to look it over, Mr. Jackson."

"Get the police first," put in the Chemist. "You can't suppress evidence of a crime."

The Doctor raised his hand. "The crime of arson presupposes a malicious firing of property with intent to defraud an insurance office. I believe that is the legal definition. We only know Mr. Jackson burned his property. We cannot say yet that it was with intent to defraud. If he reaches an immediate and satisfactory settlement with Mr. Martin, I should say we were privileged to keep our scientific records to ourselves. Of course, if he does not settle—" The Doctor's shrug was expressive and his implication exceedingly unpleasant.

"Lemme see that paper, young man," demanded Jackson.

Jimmy Martin handed it over. It was an offer of settlement of the claim for twenty-five dollars! What Jackson's innermost feelings were, one can only guess. This was a business transaction, and in business Mr. Jackson's expression was always blank.

"We are willing to pay twenty-five dollars," Martin explained, "so that there will be no implication of any—er, trouble. To spare you—you understand."

Jackson fingered the paper. "Suppose I would settle," he suggested to the Doctor. "You'd give me the pictures you took?"

"Yes," agreed the Doctor readily. "We will smash them to bits here before your eyes. Get your negatives, Mr. Jensen. I give you my word, Mr. Jackson—and I speak for all these gentlemen—that nothing of this will go beyond these walls."

Jackson nodded. A moment later, reluctantly, as though his soul were torn with anguish—as no doubt it was—he signed.

"Now them plates," he demanded.

The Photographer brought them, muttering to himself in protest. They were still wet—mere rectangles of light and shadow. He held one of them to the light, pointing out the figure of Jackson in his chair—and behind him, in the shadows, the vague, blurred outlines of a building on fire.

"Want to see any more, Mr. Jackson?"

Jackson glanced at another, which chanced to show his thoughts of that same pipe. He shuddered again and, seizing the plates, threw them to the floor and stamped them vigorously with his heel.

A few seconds later, again suavely businesslike, admitting nothing but the frank regret that he had ever ventured into the realms of science, Mr. Arthur Jackson departed.

The Doctor smiled at his friends. "You got my point quickly, gentlemen. You are clever, all of you." His approving glance went to the Lawyer particularly.

"I didn't get your point," declared the Banker. "I don't understand yet how you did it. You—you didn't actually photograph his thoughts?"

"No," and the Doctor laughed. "Of course we didn't. Jensen photographed that pipe yesterday. Martin dug it out of the ruins and brought it here. For the rest—well, they were rather clever double exposures. I had some very sketchy wash drawings made of what I thought might have occurred—very vague, you understand. They might have meant almost anything. A guilty conscience, I assumed, would interpret them properly—especially in the excitement of the moment. Jensen photographed the drawings this afternoon, and tonight, by ordinary flashlight photography, he superimposed a portrait of our late visitor on them with another exposure."

"But that weird, colored flash—" the Banker began.

"That was merely for effect. The first puff of white light made the exposure. The red light did nothing except impress Jackson."

The Doctor's smile was almost wistful as he added:

"Do you know, gentlemen, I believe we will be able to photograph thoughts someday, don't you?"

ABOUT THE AUTHOR

"HE IS A Verne returned and Wells going forward," remarked "Bob" Davis, dean of American magazine editors. "He is the American H. G. Wells," say other critics.

Cummings has an unusual flair for things scientific as evidenced by the fact that while at Princeton University he accomplished the remarkable feat of absorbing three years of physics in that many months. His five years' association with Thomas A. Edison as the latter's personal assistant also added to Cummings's scientific knowledge. His bizarre early life, living on orange plantations in Puerto Rico, striking oil in Wyoming, gold seeking in British Columbia, timber cruising in the North, before he was twenty, also left its imprint.

Leaving Mr. Edison's employ, Cummings began writing scientific fiction for many magazines. His stories gripped the popular imagination and they "clicked." Mr. Cummings's success as a writer has been meteoric, for in a few years he has become one of the world's most popular authors of scientific fiction.

Yet when asked about his own life and experiences Mr. Cummings is shy and evasive. He would much rather talk about Miss Betty Starr Cummings, his four-year-old daughter, whom he terms "the really interesting member of the family."

A few of her exploits include being wrecked and transshipped in a heavy sea; adrift with her parents in a disabled open boat when only three weeks old; traveling thousands of miles by automobile, train and steamer; weathering a Florida hurricane and coming safely through an automobile accident. From all of which we can see that Mr. Cummings leads rather an adventurous life himself!

Winter finds him at home in Bermuda, but when the temperature starts to rise he quickly makes tracks for Quebec. As we write this a letter arrives from Bermuda announcing that his next full length fantastic novel will soon be ready for *Argosy* readers.

In the office of *Fantastic Novels* the other day, Mr. Cummings looked this autobiography over with a smile. "It's all right," he said, "except that Betty is fourteen and has already sold a story of her own, which she wrote when she was thirteen. Fulton Oursler accepted it for *Liberty Magazine!*"

Asked about how he came to write "The Girl in the Golden Atom," Mr. Cummings said that it was the very first thing that he ever wrote, and that he did it simply because he felt like putting down and developing the idea of entering a world inside a ring. He had no thought of selling it, nor even that it might be a usable story. Two friends, William C. McNulty, an important American etcher, and Spring Byington, motion picture actress (known nowadays as *the mother* in "The Jones Family" on the radio) looked over the story, and liked it. Mr. Cummings, who knew no rules for writing but simply put it down "straight from the heart" read it aloud to Mr. McNulty and to Miss Byington when either of them asked how it was coming along. They were very enthusiastic and urged him to take it to a publisher. Bob Davis snapped it up.

And Ray Cummings has been writing ever since.

www.ingramcontent.com/pod-product-compliance
Lightning Source LLC
Chambersburg PA
CBHW030535030726
47495CB00004B/1001